Jo Dot is a Human Resc
member of the Chart ~~~ ui Personnel and
Development (CIPD). An interest in wellbeing at work
and mental health led Jo Dot to training in mindfulness
and alternative healing via several modalities. She is also a
qualified therapeutic practitioner in forest bathing (shinrin-
yoku). Her passions include painting large pictures,
snowboarding, slalom water-skiing, trees and crystals.

DEDICATION

The Painting is dedicated to my son Lucas and my brothers Frank and John.

JO DOT PARKER

THE PAINTING

AUSTIN MACAULEY PUBLISHERS™

LONDON • CAMBRIDGE • NEW YORK • SHARJAH

ISBN 9781528990066 (Paperback)
ISBN 9781528990073 (Hardback)
ISBN 9781528990080 (ePub e-book)

www.austinmacauley.com

First Published 2022
Austin Macauley Publishers Ltd®
1 Canada Square
Canary Wharf
London
E14 5AA

CHAPTER 1

The Morning

THE SUN'S FIRST rays had started to trickle above the horizon like pale, yellowy-gold paint, smudging its way across the night sky. Crouched in the firelight, she could just make out dark swathes of seaweed strewn at the edge of the shoreline, where she'd last seen him. It reminded her of discarded clothing that had missed the laundry basket, and the life she knew he'd outgrown.

She looked up, for a moment only conscious of her breathing. In the balmy, salty, night air, the immeasurable, star-crusted heavens seemed to reassure her that he was still alive.

Folding in half the last words he had written, and then folding them in half again, she pushed the abstract poem back into the pocket of her flimsy dress with all the other messages she had picked up. His finely patterned thinking lay all around her in the dormant scenery that he had articulated them both into. Familiar now with the words that he had previously put together, she allowed the peacefulness above her to take up the space he had been occupying in her mind. She liked that he was so unpredictable and difficult to stay one step ahead of, exhausting as it was, but she also needed her detachment. Breathing in the timeless rhythm of everything and nothing, it was a relief to be able to halt her thoughts and be free of her concern for him.

Above her, the thin fingers of gold were spreading, slowly searching, seeping into the hairline cracks of another universe, allowing her a glimpse of what it would be like not to be a part of his picture. Then it was back—a sigh of self-awareness—like a crease in the night's perfect glittering veil of order that she longed to smooth out and pretend had never been there.

It was a moment away from a job still to be done, words and thoughts to be rearranged. *Thank God for moments*, she thought, *the moments make sense of everything.* She always wished that the moments could last forever, or at least be stretched out for longer, but that was the point of her being here.

It was her turn at guarding the fire. She crouched beside it, sipping lukewarm tea, while the other women slept. They had lit it more for light than warmth. The silence was enjoyable, with nobody to respond to, interrupted only by the odd spark of firelight rocketing into the summer night air before drifting back lightly to the gritty sand that was trying to blend the pebbles. A full harvest moon, hanging like a heavy antique pendant of carved ivory, was still holding court over the shore. The piercing sparkle of Venus just below it winked softly, appearing and disappearing, as thin strands of clouds quietly drifted by. She knew that her sister, Ourania, had done her best to illuminate the contrast for what the night and the morning offered him on his journey. They had all done their best for him.

An old Spanish guitar lay where she'd left it, away from the fire, safe in the shadows. It didn't seem completely silent, as if still resonating from the notes she'd picked out when she had tuned it earlier. Adding some siren-like humming, she'd found it soothing to pick at the strings using her expertise to tighten them where they needed it. With no real tune or catchy riff emerging from her fingers, she'd set the guitar down and continued to hum quietly to herself. A misshapen treble clef, shrivelled minims, scratchy semibreves, and crotchets curling at the ends, all floated down in disappointment to settle beside the guitar before the dawn had started to break. The random sounds lay in a disorganised heap around the carefully honed wooden shape. The jumble of collapsed creativity was separated from all the broken poetic words and half-written lyrics that he couldn't be bothered with anymore, fallen into disuse, blown unsentenced across the sand, or stuck under stones waiting to be upturned. She'd managed to find several small scraps of verse and lines missing from their song or the poetry they were intended for. The folded-up bits of paper were now bulging out of her dress pocket.

The ivory moonbeams had managed to locate the guitar's lacquered, mahogany surface as soon as she'd put it down. The perfectly tightened strings seemed to be shining, tempting her to play again. She calmly observed it now as if she was looking critically at herself. She'd played those strings for many years, pressing on the wooden frets with just enough pressure to leave permanent indentations in the fingertips of her left hand. And, with her right hand, she always enjoyed picking the squeaky strings with just the right amount of intention. Playing the guitar had become a part of who she was. Even when she got the notes wrong, she was always confident that it was part of getting it right, as long as she kept trying for the sake of inspiration. But it was going to have to remain silent for a while now.

She rubbed the burnt fingertips of her left hand, still sore from trying to touch the flames. Staring into the fire, still humming, eyes half-closed, she'd been mesmerised by the fiery, unpredictable twists and curtsies. In the middle of the Terpsichorean flames she could almost see the red-haired figure of one of her sisters dancing; flashing amber eyes ablaze with the fun of it all. Unsure if it had possessed her, or been there all the time, a primaeval urge to touch the fire had shot up through her torso from wherever it had been lurking deep inside her gut. The pain had been quick and intense like a wasp sting as the flames licked her flesh, and it brought her instantly back to her senses.

The suddenness of the pain had caused her to spill the beaker of tea she'd been holding in her other hand. Drops of the tepid liquid had made the fire hiss briefly before the flames excitedly recovered their charm. She didn't like the feeling of vulnerability when she was meant to be on duty. Her resolve was instantly clear that it wasn't going to happen again. Indignant for having lost herself, she'd worked out how she would recall what happened and decided that her own humming had sent her drifting off to sleep for a split-second. She knew that was how history was made and set down.

She would have liked to sing something once the sun was up but that was unlikely now without enough words, and with burnt fingers. She'd managed well enough till recently to keep him entertained. Harmonic vibrations curdling off the guitar strings continually tempted and evoked new responses from him. With the guitar escorting his lyrics, and her voice soaring, they could set his world to rights. Thoughts and feelings falling into place as they were left behind and made insignificant by the new place that the sequence of musical notes took him to. Or they could dredge up the deepest seabed of history and fear, unearthing primitive curiosities that hadn't been imagined yet, demanding to be made real. It just depended on who was leading whom and the intention behind the lyrics. She was deft at arranging the notes, the length of time the vibrations had on the air, and the gaps between them before they reached his ears, hoping to resonate with his thinking. And in return, he was able to articulate feelings into words that she needed.

But there wasn't going to be any music today, and there were no lyrics. He hadn't provided any words for a while despite her attempts to inspire him. Retrieving it from her pocket, she unfolded the last poem he'd written and tucked under a stone. She tried hard to make sense of it. "Maybe we need a rest from each other," she mumbled to herself, reading it slowly for the third time, memorising the words.

She was content enough spending some time alone with her own thought processes, quietly sifting through recent experiences. Letting her ego find the most comfortable place to store them, she liked deciding what value and impact to let each experience have on her; what meaning to afford it in her overall purpose. If her framework of reference was her home, the soft furnishings, shapes and colour schemes had all somehow come together organically throughout her existence. Sometimes, things happened that didn't fit anywhere yet within her eclectic thinking. Because they didn't fit, she didn't notice them gathering dust in her mind until something else happened and brought them into focus.

But she needed the others to awaken now, as she gently, ceremonially, scooped small handfuls of sand onto the driftwood and settled the flames into silence. They had, anyway, just about given up spitting into what was left of the darkness. Burning, changing the blackened ensemble of driftwood washed up onto the shore, the fire had finished its performance. Smoky wisps and silent ashes mixed with sand now replaced the flickering, warm colours that had danced all night under the stars. The smell of the smoke was calming as she allowed it to enter her nostrils and merge with her breath.

The other women were starting to stir from an uncomfortable sleep. Sheltered against one of the many large sand dunes set back from the reach of the tide, topped with tufts of long, pale grasses, they had been propped up against each other as best they could for some cushioning. The undulating outline of their graceful bodies made it hard to define them separately in the dimness. All the dreams from the night carried by the tussocks of whispering grass were being yawned out one by one, forgotten and exhaled from their minds. They were all wearing long summer dresses that appeared to be of bronze and burnt russet material. But they would soon transform into peach reds and coral pinks when the growing light showed their true colours. Their co-ordinated clothing and waking movements were a perfect accompaniment to the orchestra of sunrays creeping across the summer's fading night sky. She waited patiently and started to prepare herself for them to become fully awake.

Blinking, as her eyes adjusted to the hints of dawn, she watched more thin shafts of gold gradually weaving over the still predominantly moonlit shore. The sea was quietly mirroring the altered sky, its shallow, silver-edged waves becoming more visible. The first bird's long-drawn-out warble decided to make itself heard across the grassy dunes in the distance. She felt the distinct sensation of hope as the early morning light started to fall around her golden-brown hair in a softly tangled offering of pale orange ribbons.

"Want some bread, Clio?" one of the women whispered, holding out a torn chunk of the wholesome but stale-looking loaf being passed around in a creased brown-paper bag. She looked at the bread being offered and quickly returned her eyes to stare at the changing sky.

"No thanks—leave it for the birds?" she replied with pre-occupied disinterest before adding an afterthought, "Not that the crows will eat it though. I once heard, someone said, carrion birds won't eat bread." She made a mental note to herself that what she'd just said might make a good lyric.

"How about some chocolate, then?" asked the other woman in a husky, half-asleep voice. "There's some left."

Taking a moment to work out whether the offer was intended for her or the crows, she replied softly, "I'm fine, Polly" using her sister's name to emphasise that she didn't wish to be asked again. Nonetheless, she raised an eyebrow as she imagined what the chocolate would taste like.

"Have you decided whether you're coming with us, Clio?" the husky voice continued, squinting at her with narrowed eyes, their deep green colour difficult to make out in the dusk. While she waited for a response, she attempted to shake the darkness, sand and breadcrumbs from the folds of her crumpled dress. It had wrapped itself around her ankles, biding its time. If nobody knew better it was pretending to be a dull brown but would be revealed as bright, flirty red just as soon as the morning had fully established itself. Meanwhile, with eyes remaining transfixed on the sky, head slowly shaking, the response eventually came,

"No—I can't leave yet."

The rest of the women stopped their almost choreo-graphed yawning, stretching, hair-grooming and looked sympathetically towards her. The deep green eyes and seven other beautiful, sleepy faces stared at her in the half light. A treasure chest of assorted jewels, all turned in her direction. Glints of sapphires, brown ambers, blue and gold topaz, tuorquoise, and emeralds, starting to adjust to the new day, watched her from different angles. She knew there were sudden thoughts firing between their minds, flicking faster than time itself through millions of memories, snapshots.

Standing up, she tensed her body and tilted her chin towards the sky to show them she wasn't interested in listening. She wanted to shield herself from their influence and be sure her thoughts were her own, wondering why they cared and why she needed to know that they did. At the same time, she was aware that she would be feeling different if she wasn't being reminded of the connective presence they shared. It could be felt, strengthening and reinforcing her like scaffolding, but she wanted to be free of the need to respond. The last thing she wanted was for any of them to start trying to articulate how they were feeling. That would require her to contribute the right responses, to support the moment, and she just didn't have the presence of mind for it. Grateful that none of them was fully awake, she pretended to rub the sleep from her eyes and faked a yawn. "I know it's been nearly two years, but I don't think he's going to give in. He's still on the shore somewhere."

In the several silent seconds that lapsed, computations threaded through the conduits of historic exchanges stored in their minds. Experiences they had shared and inherited. Immature reactions, unidentified emotions without any clear causes or triggers. All sifted somewhere in the past, they had attached themselves to memories as they settled and found their place in the sands of time. It was their version of a story until anyone cared to rewrite it and make them remember it differently. Her seeming detachment to the bonds between them stirred up whirling panic that the others struggled to compose. Thoughts streamed incoherently. They anxiously realised there wasn't time to re-examine the memories—like multi-faceted crystals in the changing light—or prepare responses. They would certainly have enjoyed that.

She held her breath and waited, as if everything that wasn't being said was too much for her. She'd robbed them of the pleasure of untangling the impact of their own stories and envies impressed on the history they all shared. There wasn't time to arrive at refined decisions or uncover the real reason for their reactions, all there in the mess "somewhere" that history had tried to tidy up for the sake of getting on with things.

They were looking forward to the day, assuming it would be spent in a new direction, separating to search along the shoreline, and then coming together again. The best part was coming together to share their experiences and ideas and to build a new campfire. It was how they usually were, setting out as sisters, parting to search during the day, resting with each other at night, lighting fires and talking into the darkness until they fell asleep. The talking, comparing, consensus, and decision-making was all hard work. Sleeping, dreams, sifting and interpreting created history to enable the next day and the possibility of having to re-interpret it. Wandering in and out of each other's dreams, browsing the surreal and the abstract, their ideas sought shape and form. Returning to the same spot now for several nights, they had just patiently assumed that her interest in him had waned. They hadn't anticipated that she really might give him another chance after all the long, protracted discussion the night before about moving on when the sun rose.

It was all just too fast for them to properly comprehend or attempt to influence when they weren't even fully awake. Words failed to form as a few silly tears brimmed on some of their beautiful eyelids, and affection for her poured into their hearts. Caught off-guard, their reactions betrayed the purpose of disappointment as it punctured through to their inert feelings and sense of identity. A few moments more, and their synchronised, protective instincts gave sway to the respect they held for each other's right to experience where their curiosity took them. Their sisterly connections started to re-tune, conscious of their over-arching need to remain free to inspire, unbridled by commitment to precedent and assumptions. Calm was restored. She let out a deep breath and her body relaxed again as she felt the cacophony of feelings subsiding back to the safety of a well-rehearsed script.

Eventually, the green eyes smiled at her. "I understand. It happened to me too once—do you remember? I wasn't able to explore anything else either. But it's exhausting and, in the end, I wished I'd moved on a bit sooner. You can't stay here forever. It's torturous."

"I know," she said, crouching back down to the extinguished driftwood, still enjoying the smell of its warm, ashy crumble, rubbing it between her burnt fingertips to salve the pain. She turned her gaze towards the sympathetic voice. She was grateful that the bonds between them were being left unspoken, with everything kept in its place. She would try to understand what she was feeling later in her own time, think about them, examine the memories like a photo album.

She would miss the other women as much as they would miss her when they were a safe distance away.

"Well," said another of them, "if you really think it's not over, I guess he'll be here soon, so we should be going."

"You might as well take my guitar," she said quietly. "I'm not going to be able to play it for a while—I got too close to the fire and..." she hesitated, "...he's been very quiet lately." Seeing their immediate concern, she licked her burnt fingertips to show them there was no serious damage. "He's made me realise we're too hung up about words anyway," she continued with a look of introspective intrigue, widened eyes staring at nothing in particular. "I mean, words aren't even an original language—just tools to process and connect our thoughts and information, right?"

The green eyes squinted, plunged deep into thought, fished around for a moment and then yawned again, not quite ready to accept the day yet.

"Not sure how that would affect our creativity but I'll think about it." And then, quickly finishing the yawn, the emerald eyes laughed, "Without words in mind, of course."

She accepted their embraces as they took it in turns to kneel beside her to say their goodbyes. Wrapping their arms tightly around her, pressing their heads against her body as if to check that she was still breathing, stroking her hair, kissing her head, they prepared themselves to leave.

Their chattering and pleasantries, kisses and hugs swirled around her in the morning air like perfume as she remained crouched beside the extinguished fire. She didn't rise to her feet again as they made a last, polite attempt to persuade her to start walking with them, extending their hands towards her with sisterly smiles. It was disconcerting to not all be setting off together, but they could see that her thoughts were somewhere else, arrested by the changing scenery under the lightening heavens. It felt strange already to be without them, but she wondered if the aloneness might just make all the difference. They left her with the remains of the bread and some squares of chocolate wrapped in gold foil.

Not wishing to delay the pursuit of their own interests any longer, they continued to untangle their hair, wriggled the sand out from between their toes, and straightened their clothing. One of them picked up her guitar, insisting they would find their way back to her when she had satisfied herself as to what this morning had to offer.

They started to head in an easterly direction along the shore where the sun was now evidently rising on the day. Their steps were slow at first as they began to find their pace, negotiating the shingle and lapping sea. Each of them remembered to turn and wave back at various points as they went.

As they walked away, their long sunrise-coloured dresses became more apparent, colours fluttering around their bodies, blurring them into the half-lit shoreline. Their chatter brightened on the topic of creativity and their delight with being part of the scenery. Their voices only lowered to whisper, in agreement, how convinced they were that nothing was going to change, their belief that he was spent—and how this day would be no different. She watched them, walking together in a huddle with their dresses gently billowing in the light breeze off the waves, till eventually they blended to look like a flock of strange pink birds in the growing light.

Strains of warmth had begun to outline the scene with sharper edges. The moon wobbled a little in and out of focus as if contemplating a struggle to hold off the day. She sighed, relieved to be alone, picked up the brown paper bag, breaking up what was left of the bread inside before turning it upside down and sprinkling the crumbs into the air for the birds. Remembering the chocolate, she peeled back the foil, broke off a square and allowed herself to be distracted by its perfect texture. It became impossibly smooth as it dissolved between the warmth of her tongue and the roof of her mouth with just the right amount of adhesion. Whatever thoughts and whatever reality she was wrestling with, the taste of chocolate was undeniable in the silence.

When the other women had disappeared from view, the twilight moistened with a brief drizzle and the rusty smell of summer rain. She wasn't completely surprised by the indication that he was pondering whether to wash over and repaint the sky.

CHAPTER 2

The Artist

S HE DIDN'T NEED to look to know he was approaching. His fine brushstrokes were conducting a light, salty breeze to blow in time with the dark green sea that had started to roll gently back and forth over the sand, the stones, and the washed-up shells. Her haloed hair fluttered like a thousand excited golden threads caught alight in the dawn of his new thoughts.

She turned her gaze to the distance where the artist walked, head hung low, while he rhythmically waved a slender paintbrush in the air, curly wisps of youthful, black hair obscuring his boy-blue eyes, and his feet beginning to falter. Even when she couldn't see him, she knew how far he had come. She knew when he was going to appear in one of her days. She knew when he needed her long before he could possibly realise it himself.

He stopped and placed the paintbrush behind his right ear while he looked to see what he could make out along the shore to catch his imagination. One hand went to his forehead in the way that people shield their eyes to see better, looking as best he could into the hazy mix of sun trying to burn off the moonlight, hitting the wet sand where the waves repeatedly rolled away. He smiled weakly, shifting his feet a little more apart to steady himself. He instantly elicited her protective instincts. If she hadn't been watching him at that particular moment, the words from his most recent poem wouldn't suddenly have made sense to her. Her mouth opened as she pulled the note from her pocket and unfolded it again, whispering to herself, "He doesn't realise he's writing about something he can't see."

> *Turning in sunlight you dare*
> *to lose your balance squinting;*
> *and your frail smile so unaware*
> *of the exposure taking place,*
> *forgets the fossilised damage.*

He'd come a long way since she'd first spotted him. Stretched out behind his tall, slim silhouette, a trail of shells and small stones deposited or dropped here and there in the sand, along with his sea-washed footprints, were testimonies to his decision-making. He stopped looking into the distance and picked up another stone which was wet, polished smooth by waves and moonlight. Then he walked a few more paces, head bent and shoulders tensed, in the early morning light searching the damp sand, stones, and crunchy sounds beneath his feet. Rubbing the stone dry against his grubby, grey jeans, he passed it from one hand to the other, running his fingertips against his palms to remove the little wedges of grit and sand from under his nails. He didn't notice the gentle landing behind him of a sooty black crow, active in its dawn patrol for food. It quickly surveyed the shingle, now glowing in the early hues of sunrays, lit like a huge carpet of tumbled rose quartz spread out for him to walk on.

The gleaming sunlit shingle was punctuated around the crow's landing with wet breadcrumbs and a selection of moist, glistening shells from razorfish, limpets, mussels and all sorts. The crow, head to one side, hopping, inspecting, appeared to possess an ability to appreciate the intricacy of the grooves and aesthetics under its claws. It picked up a cracked length of razor shell in its beak, only to make sure it was empty of life and it hadn't missed anything. If the artist had seen how comically the crow had flung the razor shell in disgust at finding it empty, before decisively twisting its head in the opposite direction, he might have come close to laughing. Then the bird lifted itself energetically back into the warm, moist morning breeze, not wishing to rest on the disappointment of finding nothing more substantial to eat than a few pappy breadcrumbs. The artist didn't appear to have noticed, but the woman saw it and smiled. The idea of a crow with an eye for art and beauty beyond the mortal purpose of design—and maybe a sense of humour—would last longer than most thoughts she'd had recently. "Thalia would have loved this" she thought, missing her sisters just a little, recalling the importance of fun and knowing that Thalia would be finding ways to keep the rest of them laughing despite their disappointment that she had wanted to stay behind.

She sat down and continued to watch the artist getting used to the new day and finding his way. Her original interest in him had returned periodically to his eccentric uncertainty as he had set out to walk along the shoreline. His faltering footsteps somehow caught between land and water without commitment to either. His walk of indecision saw him tripping frequently or stopping to stare out to sea, sighing sadly at the sight of speeding boats and people at play on the waves. His assumption that everyone was complete and happy made him feel something was missing in his life. Something he had to find or understand first before he could wade out into a world he observed and analysed but couldn't imagine being a part of again.

He wasn't the first person to find himself stranded on the shore, trying to realise who he wanted to be and how he had got there. He wasn't the first artist she had tried to help understand the fear-filled sensation of nothing where he felt "something" should be. She couldn't be sure yet. But maybe it was his dissatisfaction with drifting from day to day, or his lack of interest in other people, that had increased her attention on him.

Deep inside his chest, he could feel a space where the "something" was meant to fit. His need for order and his ability to smell patterns had taken over the self-regulating mechanics of his brain which he couldn't be bothered to use anymore. He was bored, on autopilot, and he was afraid of what that did to him as he explored the surreal more deeply. He believed there had to be something that would interest him, save him and seal off the passage of his curiosity into a dimension that didn't allow him to function. Searching for clues inside the shells and under the stones had grown from a mild distraction to an almost constant pastime. Before each tomorrow that she helped him into, she hoped that the safe, dark and damp inertia under the stones would finally become the perfect contrast for him to appreciate the smell of rain, the warmth of the sun on his face and the breeze through his hair. She longed to see him deeply inhaling the air that his lungs were intended for in the world he had been born to live in.

This morning, she had the feeling that something was about to change. It was that feeling that saw her resist the urge to join the other women. It was an excitement that she thankfully had no interest in analysing. When it came to art that appealed to her, she never had to understand why it was of interest. Why she became so excited by certain arrangements of colour, line and composition remained a mystery and was beyond her gift to explain. She just loved what she loved, and it was at its best when she didn't have to dismantle it in discussion with the others. She believed that some things were for the experience of her mind and her mind alone, without interference from her temporal reasoning. She was the ideal muse for him. He slowed and took in the same rain-misted, dawn sky that was intriguing her. As his eyes trailed the distance, he spotted her watching him. He'd been wondering when she would appear. He noticed that she wasn't carrying the guitar. Rather than spending too long wondering why it wasn't with her, he felt relieved. She was glad she had decided to stay in his picture a little longer.

Back along the shoreline, somewhere he'd find it impossible to pinpoint, he'd tired of his imagination. It became too obvious to him that if he wanted the sky to be green he could paint a picture of it, but that it wouldn't change the sky. There were no limits to his imagination, but he'd hit boundaries in his reality. He'd stopped enjoying the scenery and had started to re-examine what he was painting. He was unsure of why he was walking, searching, or what it was that he wanted to find; overwhelmed by everything he could hope for. He knew things were meant to be different, and he knew he could change his picture, rearrange what was at his disposal. What he wasn't quite sure of was exactly what he wanted to change it to, under a sky that was always ideally intended to be blue.

And now, with the distance between them narrowing, his steps slowed, hesitating again. A smile settled across her soft face as she surveyed the trail where hope had managed to tease him this far. She was delighted to see that he had almost caught up with her, the gap narrowing just a fraction on each moment that they shared. The closer he got, the more she enjoyed being a part of his creativity and the assortment of finely crafted items that tumbled out of his mind. Even if he himself had become bored with it, she most definitely appreciated his imagination. *He's hard work,* she thought, *almost painful to be with at times, but...* She stopped herself knowing she was well rewarded.

She was always particularly thrilled by the shiny black crows that landed so amusingly around him every time he stooped to select another stone or shell embedded in the sand. It used to make her instantly start to pick at the guitar strings, waiting for lyrics to form to help him appreciate the crows from her perspective. Hopping with the uneasy grace of women dragging rustling black ball gowns around, they were always curious to see what he had in his hands. Their beady shamanic eyes would peer sideways with the eager anticipation of fun—wanting to play—and hopeful for a tiny meaty morsel of shellfish from whatever he had picked up. He enjoyed their interruptions but never quite knew how to respond when they appeared. Responsible for painting them there, he had nothing to feed them and had somehow forgotten how to have fun. So, he and the crows ended up sharing awkwardness with each other every time they met, despite the repeated attraction.

His picture had become increasingly static with contrast. Bouts of desperation and joy, confidence and doubt, all painted so strongly that they cancelled each other out. He was trying to function in cognitive dissonance but struggling to blur the edges of the contrast for the colours to bleed into each other. Toying with decisions about whether and where to increase the richness of the colour, tone it down or wash over it completely, breathing in and rejecting life as he thought about perspective and definition, light and shadow.

Until this morning, it was the familiarity with the static tension of indecisive contrast that had prevented him from scrubbing everything out and starting again. Ambivalent, he'd become fearful of familiarity as it tried to define him with the way people saw him in its context. In the way he thought of himself, and in the way his behaviour turned into habits that took on an identity of their own. Fearful and anxious about the same old things, the taste of hope on his tongue was stale. A scrap of bread when there was nothing else to eat. Familiarity made him feel alienated from himself and, at the same time, safe. The endless taunt of something else to make familiar enough to want to grow away from, both intrigued him and scorched his thoughts like a moth to a flame. But he'd run out of interest, knew all the scripts and responses that were acceptable to the familiar which increased its limitations.

He'd battled on like a true artist, wrestling with whether or not to create something that didn't already exist. Uncertain of whether he had any real talent for it. If there were well-trodden paths ahead, the footprints of role models had been kept hidden from him, washed away by the sea. It was just as well. Wrestling with uncertainty felt significantly better in his mind than not having enough identity to start working out the next steps. Unable to see where he was, he had arrived where only change could provide the new definition he desperately sought. He'd reached that point where he'd have to break free of the static to prevent his mind from cracking with indecision. The contrast had forced him to at least be clear about what he didn't want as it continued to form a blockade between his imagination and reality. Dissatisfied with painting to replicate how he saw the landscape in front of him, he was going to have to create what he needed to survive the gravitational pull of not making a decision. The continuation of his indecision, he realised, was becoming an even bigger decision in itself, and if nothing changed, he would stay the same.

The woman raised her angular chin. Her fine nostrils flared a little in the morning air. At last—this was what she had been waiting for. This was why their need for each other had become more intense as he'd struggled to paint with his contrasting ideas. She held her breath again but this time with anticipated delight.

This was not the careful weighing up or erosion of options, not quite curiosity and not quite necessity. What would result from it would be more important than what he was letting go of, and that was all he needed to do. Insofar as true artists have no choice in the matter, any notion to stop painting altogether wasn't sustainable. In comparison, change felt right, so it couldn't be wrong. He felt something close to being ready to paint again.

CHAPTER 3

The Stone

HE ROLLED HIS shoulders in an attempt to ease a familiar tension that had crept in over the many days that had merged into what he now thought of as his life. Even when he awoke from the semblance of sleep, his shoulders still ached. He was aware of her—the woman—always ahead when he saw her, stopping every now and then to watch him from the distance. Sometimes, it was difficult to know whether she was facing towards him or away from him, silhouetted in the rising and setting colours on the shore. Then, only the way she was holding the guitar to one side of her body gave him a clue. Her presence had drawn him like a compass point and, even when he didn't see her for several days, he knew she'd be back—his muse. It helped him in the frightening return to his life each morning. Frantically assembling and shuffling the deck of cards he'd been handed to find just one to help him take a second breath. One card with a perspective of hope to stop his eyes from closing again, propping his eyelids open. And the first glimpse of the woman when she returned had become reassuring as their need for each other grew.

She and the rest of the women had watched others walk this coastline and admit defeat long before now, as they settled for being able to say that they had tried. Some had insisted that whatever they found and picked up from the shore was special and just exactly what they were looking for, even when, in that place deep inside, they knew it wasn't. Always, their ability to imagine beyond the familiar was trapped within the gravitational force of their perception of reality. Sparks of discontent had shown in every step they took, projected on everyone they resented, self-perpetuating the familiar with their refusal to engage with the present. One or two figured that if they kept rejecting what wasn't right, it could only leave what they were looking for—but it hadn't. They thought about what they no longer wanted, and how discontent it made them but they didn't seem able to imagine what the relief would feel like. Others who walked along the shore simply changed or traded their priorities, coming close to having their hopes realised, merely to say it wasn't what they wanted after all, when they were unable to tolerate the hope any longer. Or maybe they were just unable to cope with the identity crisis of actually having what they wanted. A fearful number of them had given in, returning to the safety of dull conversation that made no real connections. Some would come to wonder how disappointment had adjusted their expectations to such an extent that they found comfort in boredom. Perplexed that their effort might make no difference, they had fitted into the picture they were trying to avoid without actually really being a part of it. Others continued to make use of hope to adapt or modify their approach without giving up on what they said they wanted. If they got it right, they liked how it changed them. Somewhere along the shoreline, they all came to realise what they would settle for, and it determined how they would grow old from that point onward. It was progress for the few that truly felt as if the last grain of sand had peacefully fallen through the glass timer into its rightful place. But for those that came to a halt, slowed down by the weight of everybody else's perception of where they should be, it felt like defeat. Finding it harder to walk across the large, flat and squidgy patches of sand nearest to the sea, they stumbled up the shore onto the stones and shingle, irritated by every step until they dropped to their knees. Other people's stories set to music repeatedly drumming like a vibrating wall of sound, wanting to bend minds and time, swept enough doubt into their hearts to stop them living. The usual rhythm of the tides, waves, night and day became unable to breathe energy back into them. Creative thoughts were quick to vanish on the wind of too many voices that thought they knew better, needing to justify their existence. The sighing of disappointed muses was a constant sound heard on the breeze created by the waves as they crusaded onto the shore.

The woman and her sisters had watched with the pain of intolerable patience for any mere mortal as, one by one, artist after artist laid their paintbrushes to rest along the shoreline. Patrolling the line between land and sea, they had experienced too many times those who were unable to realise that it was impossible to change what they couldn't accept in the first place. The way "this becomes that", and how "that doesn't exist without this", both inspired and eluded them like the distant and uncertain relationship between the muse and her artist.

Her eyebrows were now arched above her wide, expectant gaze. *He was different*, she thought. She hadn't been wrong. Her head tingled as if a fly was crawling gently over her skull. His creativity and his strange instinct with pattern told him that the missing "*something*" was on the shore. He had to find it because whenever he caught a glimpse of the woman it sparked a memory of having painted it. After all, it was still his picture. He had assumed that he would know it when he saw it.

He'd thought about putting his brush down for good, several times. It might have given him some temporary respite to let go, to give in to the evidence laid down in the history of others. Evidence that said he should have given up by now. He could have. He'd tried to visualise being content with fulfilling the perceptions of people who didn't paint. Curious as to how he would function now that he'd given up the habit of hope, if not hope itself, he wondered what would fall into place around him to provoke his survival instincts. If painting sometimes made him feel that he was having a never-ending tantrum inside a plastic bag, it was worse to be flooded with the nothingness of having to accept that he would never paint again. It was an image that just didn't appear to be filed anywhere in his head. He didn't know how to do that and still exist. It was that simple; nothing really too impressive.

The woman hadn't been able to give up either, attracted by his struggle. In the increasing sunlight, she watched him halt to stare anxiously out across the sea, nervously twisting the stone he had picked up between his shaky fingers, and she knew. He could feel with the nail of his middle finger where the stone had been slightly chipped, disguised with grains of sand filling the notch. So, it wasn't as smooth as he'd thought, but, *No matter*, he thought. People would wonder what was so special about this stone. It was small, flattened, irregular but vaguely triangular with curves where the corners might have been. The notch was just along one of the edges between two of the indications of corners. He could fit his thumb neatly into a comfortable dip on one side. An offering from somewhere deep in the earth, he wouldn't know how long it had taken to form or make its way to the shore for him. How many thousands, millions and even billions of years were held in its molecular structure was not important to him, but he was soothed by the subtle vibration of warmth building in his hand. Smooth shades of brown, it was glistening bronze with the residue of seawater reflecting the morning light and a stripe of golden yellow revealing itself when he looked at it from certain angles.

She imagined what the other women would say. Some might guess that the truth lay in the split-second when the stone had become special because it had fulfilled the role of being found. That it had been found because his ability to tolerate any more confusion or uncertainty in the contrast was spent, and this particular stone was just there at the time. Others might wonder if the little notch in the stone had resonated with how he saw himself and given it an identity. It was in his hand. He'd held it for long enough to infuse it with the warmth of his beliefs and feelings. Or maybe its atoms were packed so close together that it had started to feel unusually dense and significant for its size and that it had managed to capture his mind's focus? The subtle difference in the energy of the density discerned by his focus might have deluded him into making up what he needed to? Or maybe that subtle energy set up an effect? Others might guess that this small stone was special, that it had always been special to him and it was only a question of finding it through the illusion of time. That it was only time that could provide such a sense of achievement and justify the purpose of hope. He wondered if he'd just lost it previously and if maybe it had always belonged to him. So, some might say it was about timing and the predetermined and natural exhaustion of coinciding forces. A few might say it was about giving up and others might say it was about being ready. The artist might say it was just his memory putting things back into place. The woman knew that none of these tiresome twists of the mind watching itself was quite right. The vibration between him and the stone had just become clearer as his confusion had drawn him closer to his unbreakable connection with it. But the twists had brought him to a place of wanting to shake all the guesses from his head like dust, obscuring the freedom he now felt in his final detachment from everything that belonged to other people. It was a very comfortable feeling achieved by making a connection to more than himself in resonance with the stone. Right now, his thoughts didn't matter. They had kept him hopeful and fearful, searching in a never-ending singularity of separation and reunion that he could now clearly see were the same thing. He was here now, and he and the brown and yellow stone had a bond. He didn't feel able to put it down again and couldn't think of any reason to.

The outline of the moon was still very much visible but continuing to fade, slowly. Sunlight was taking over the sky, and for the first time in a long time, he watched it define everything around him. If his thinking stopped him from knowing who he was, he, at least, knew where he was. He could feel the sand and shingle that he stood on, still cool from the night through the soles of his thin canvas beach shoes. His lungs breathed the salty air that kept him alive. He was grateful that he didn't have to think about that before his mind completely stilled momentarily. He felt so present for that briefest moment in the physicality of his body, while he held the stone, that it removed all his apprehension. A soft, chewy toffee-like feeling of being completely joined up took command of him. It was for just a few seconds that defied logic, but it was all he needed to experience. The millions of years that had formed the stone allowed him to transfer and process what he might otherwise have continued to avoid; the life force in his fingers holding the regular arrangement of atoms bonded together in their crystalline structure. The shift gave him a momentary memory – a place to begin with and to know he could always find his way back to now that he had felt it. As fleeting as a moment is, it was packed with an appreciation of everything he had become through the accumulation of his experiences, his responses to them, and his decisions—and his indecision. "I couldn't be anyone else," he found himself saying out loud, seeing what a contradiction in terms it would be if he didn't like and accept himself. A rush of excitement about the day ahead quickened his pulse. The stone had been in his hand for a while now, his thumb pad enjoying the contact with its smooth surface. It had become special to him. He looked at it in his palm and thought at length about how ceremonies, symbols, adornments, and tribal dances all bore testament to the beliefs of people.

He wondered whether the symbols might actually be the beliefs and what would happen to the beliefs without the words and ceremonies. He was unable to see how beliefs that weren't born out of fear would actually manage to exist without words to think with. It occurred to him that he might not need beliefs, and that life might be fine with just knowledge, the usual appetites and needs—and the fears of being separated from them.

He tried sounding the shape of each letter that formed the words "All is well", first with his voice and then inside his head. The sound of "is" reverberated tangibly in his throat and his chest more than the fuller sound of "all" collecting at the back of his mouth, and more than the gentler sound of "well" which seemed to blow outward into the air from his lips like a wish made on a dandelion. He felt like the muse's guitar, a musical instrument having to find its own notes to unlock how he wanted to feel in the future. Some of his new thoughts were producing sounds that built up and resonated differently to how he normally felt. He decided that he had a distinct liking for the sound of "g", "h", "mmm" and all the vowels. Unsure whether it made a difference, he knew there must surely be some energy or vibration produced in his head from just thinking the words. The new thoughts, working in harmony with other thoughts he hadn't explored, finding points that resonated and started to change his tune. He asked himself if an "a" might produce a different chemical signal to a "z" as it crossed his synapses and whether "*All is well*" produced different energy to "*Todo está bien*". He tried both, imagining trying to comfort somebody in either language, and contented himself that the intention felt the same. He wondered where those words that just dropped gently into his mind, whispered around his ears, or floated up from his sleep came from. He wondered about the usefulness of words and thinking beyond the everyday problem-solving requirement to survive.

Then a match struck alight against the criss-cross of thoughts stacking up in his mind; igniting his appreciation for words again. There were so many of them and so few used. When he'd finished thinking, he folded his fingers around the stone and closed his eyes. Then he feverishly tucked it safely into the front pocket of his jeans, rubbed and clapped his hands together, and pulled the brush from behind his ear.

CHAPTER 4

The Storm

I T HAD TAKEN him a while to recover enough to follow the woman after the storm—a storm like nothing he had previously experienced. The evening hadn't given any warning before it succeeded in taking his breath away. A gradient of blue sky joined to the even bluer sea, getting ready for the blazing orange ball of gas and fire to start sinking between them. It was an invitation he couldn't resist, privileged to have the best view it was possible to have, seated comfortably with his back against the warm, pleasantly rough surface of the rock that his speedboat had been moored to. Gleaming yellow with dark blue rimming the sides, it was a beautiful example of engineering that made him happy whenever he found the time to admire it. He'd ritualistically ensured the rope had been expertly knotted and wrapped several times around the rock that wasn't ever going to move. With its historic accumulation of dark grey mineral deposits that no human eye could ever notice happening, the rock had become something of a landmark for his life and the anchor for his boat. The engine off, its passive motion was hypnotic in the gentle lapping of the sun-kissed sea, turning to orangeade in the pending sunset. He could just see the tip of his slalom ski, lying lengthways, idle across the hull. Its deep cerise colour was an appetising contrast for the orange-tinged water and glowing sunset. The delicious, warm blue and orangeade was tantalising to the impossibility of skiing, with nobody to tow him across it. All the skiers had long gone home. There was nobody around wanting him to take them out on the sea. Nobody he might persuade to drive the boat for him.

The conditions were almost uncontrollably perfect for skiing. He imagined carving the ski edge into the smooth, orange-gold liquid, a satisfying zip of water spraying into the humid summer air as the boat pulled him like a speeding pendulum repeatedly back and forth across its wake. The irony of the water being at its stillest first thing in the morning and at the end of the day, when he was alone, made him smile to himself. *No matter*, he thought, trying to enjoy the quiet isolation instead, and pondering on the need for two people. His boat, the rock, the sea and the fireball could have been the props for the final scene of another idyllic day. He could have sat, waited and watched the sun's slow descent, with swallows dashing, calling and swooping above him, living and breathing in the moment. But he had allowed himself the indulgence of feeling he could never be 'there' as long as he was 'here' and that 'this' would always prevent him being 'that'. Unable to appreciate or accept where he was, impatient to escape, the warm colours of the evening's relative perfection and beauty overwhelmed him.

It was a spontaneous decision to gather up his paints and brushes and take the boat out towards the horizon before the sun disappeared, capture how it made him feel, and somehow harness it, become a part of it, without really knowing how. The unsteadiness of the boat excited him as he stepped down into its hull and settled into the driver's seat. Prising off the lid of a large white plastic provisions box beside the passenger seat, he made a quick spot of the cans of Coke, Bourbon biscuits and packets of crisps before he pressed the lid back on. "All present and correct", he smiled. Then he put his hands on the steering wheel as if to imagine what it would feel like once he had turned the engine on. A few seconds more were spent staring out across the orange sea and the wonderful tangerine fuzziness in the air. He considered whether he could tolerate remaining on the shore that evening with nothing but his own company, undefined by anyone else, after the sun had set.

Staying still long enough to start seeing himself was something he'd never been very good at. He hated feeling trapped within the walls of his own mind, thoughts aching, tasteless like a chewed gum he needed to spit out. He already knew the answers to the array of problems trying to attract his attention. He knew how all the stories ended and how they would make him feel. All the words inside his brain were sounding like a dead language that didn't make sense to him anymore. He'd outgrown himself—hadn't spoken properly to anyone for days—but couldn't acknowledge it. He shook his head, shuddered at the thought of the options, the ordinariness, and turned the key with a defiant commitment.

He'd stopped thinking in words, wanting to get away from himself and be a part of everything that was outside of his body. The urge to be turned inside out and not exist like this was appealing. Maybe that was why he felt himself responding so intensely to the warm spectrum around him and its unspoken language of pulsating energy, permeating his cells with colour and heat, reminding him that he was alive, connecting with him and asking for nothing.

And now, the lure of the setting sun, tinting his face with its golden warmth, soothed all the aches in his mind and gave him a sense of belonging. As he adjusted the driver's mirror to make sure he would be able to check the disappearing land behind him, he caught his own reflection. His boyish blue eyes stared back at him, reflecting the sea and the sky. He grinned, shaking the curls of his unruly collar-length black hair that hadn't been combed in days. "Just what do I think I'm doing?" he laughed. Then he laughed again at his use of words, annoying midges, to question the sense of his intention, and his need to be free of them in a place where they were irrelevant.

He'd driven at top speed, carefree, excited, with the boat rhythmically bouncing off the dense surface tension of the water and smacking hard down onto it again. There was no real plan other than to get away from where he was, be as close as he could to where the sky and sea met, drift and spend some time painting the setting sun, be there and capture it. And be different. It was one of those wonderful crazy ideas that felt so right that he was swept along by his own excitement. One of those ideas that meant he wouldn't have to worry about whether he should be doing something else or be anywhere other than having the unfamiliar experience that the boat was speeding towards. He felt grown-up, fully alive, anticipating that he would soon feel a sense of belonging to the life he wanted to live instead of just admiring it.

The flaming ball in the sky didn't get any closer but the blue of the water now completely turned to gold, rippled with red and orange as the shore became more distant. The beauty of it all swallowed him and slowed him down, dazed by the colours that were refracting around him as the boat ploughed through them. He wanted to tell somebody about it, share the experience, and watch another pair of eyes glow with excitement to give him confirmation. With his sight still on the horizon, he set the boat to cruise, working out the best place to cut the engine and to start his painting while the colours were so perfect and mouth-watering.

Where he was seemed as good a place as any. Switching the engine off to let the boat drift, he cursed. He had all the paints and brushes with him but had forgotten the canvas. "Well, that was clever," he said out loud. Standing up in the boat to search for something to paint on, he wobbled slightly, and a stray thought shot through his mind as he caught hold of the side of the boat. It struck him that if he fell overboard, or something else happened that he couldn't foresee, there was nobody to pull him back aboard. The "something else" was soon drawn to his attention when he noticed the fuel gauge telling him that he could have done with gassing up before he'd left the land. Too many practicalities were now starting to spoil the view that wasn't going to stay as it was forever. Searching under wetsuits and skis for paper or cardboard to paint on, the boat was drifting from its perspective and the colours were changing. He started to wish he wasn't alone.

The cobalt-blue evening sky streaming with colours muddled from the seraphim ball of fire had been turned rapidly into an unforeseen storm. It had begun brooding before he had been able to think about bringing the boat around.

It didn't take long for cold waves to have surged up from

the deepest, disturbed laws of the ocean. The setting sun slid below the horizon and melted into the seawater, gold oil slicks to be stirred and whisked up by the dramatic change in the weather. Without another boat in sight, he was suddenly at the mercy of a leaden sky weighted with dirty laundry it wanted to toss out into the sea. Long, thin spikes of grey, pencilled rain had fallen heavily, like a bereft and sobbing soul, intent on disrupting everything that didn't share its pain. The harder he fought for control to steady the drifting boat with the roughening waves crashing around him, the further the boat dropped, submerged, and was thrown up again. Nausea, panic and disorientation took their toll on his aloneness capsizing his efforts as he lost his balance and hit his head.

He never knew how long he had spent in the sea because it didn't stack up with his understanding of time. There was a recollection of large fragments of what had happened to him as if he had experienced it in a slower, different version of time. He could still feel how desperate he had been to find something larger than his life and buoyant enough to cling to. The fragments of memory, wrecked shapes went spinning past his sinking body, his paintbrushes floating, twirling, around him. In his dream-like state he swam after one of them, making several attempts as his effort to reach it pushed it further out of his grasp. Somehow, he managed to snatch it back firmly. Clutching the brush, he gave in to drifting, sinking, till he settled on the seabed. He was drawn down as deep as it was possible to go; all the rules of life bent into the nonsense of a bad dream. He thought he could live there, unconnected to thoughts, surrendered, swirling in a green and blue abstract that couldn't support any thinking. With so much pulling him down, he could forget the life he'd been living. Where the pressure of the depths dissolved the laws of logic it was peaceful and quiet. But he knew he was drowning as he clutched his brush and focused on nothing else other than trying not to let go of it.

In his dream, he surrendered to the roller coaster of the storm tossing him back into a reality that he couldn't commit to, then dragging him down again to the intriguing, heavy depths, connected to nothing he knew. Large stately fish with heavy scales, and seductive sirens evoking new feelings and curiosity, were swimming around where he couldn't live and didn't belong. The chilliness of this unknown world set up an eerie vibration in his dislodged mind. Frozen tears started to form, rising upwards from his eyes and past him to the surface, suffocating him with a large shadow as they formed into an ice floe above. He murmured a prayer to be rescued from the dark depths of pressure that cracked through the icy watery scene and spat him back up to the surface, dashing him against a cluster of rocks. Clinging to the clammy feeling of cold grittiness gave him some brief hope before his tired hands let go of the slippery rocks to be churned back into the powerful movement of the sea, swapping the brief sensation of relief for despair.

When he had opened his eyes again, he experienced the intense disbelief of his body lying, face turned to the side, on the cold shingle, stones and wet sand where he'd washed-up on the edge of the shore. He ran his right hand over the stoniness beneath him to check that it was real. The simplicity of the physical shape of shingle, taste of salt and sand in his mouth and cold wind on his face felt good. But his sense of relative safety was gradually replaced with disturbing feelings of fear and failure. Damn feelings. He knew he could choose not to feel them. But, without being clear about what he wanted instead, his mind formed a vacuum that filled with all the worst possible doubts, attracted by the vulnerability of his predicament.

The salty sea texture was slimy as he vomited it up from his stomach and gasped in the sharp cold air he was designed to breathe. He was still clutching the paintbrush in his left hand as he lay there between worlds, the salty waves trying to take him back again, licking his feet and calves. Each roll of the seawater replayed the crash in his mind, repeated attempts to join the horizon dashed and returned to the shore. The relentless saline riff played him over and over again, shaping his reactions, exhausting his anxiety, until he finished processing what had happened and settled into calm shock at still being alive. He laid there, exhausted, with his breathing steadying—just another tumbled stone among all the other pebbles, polished by his collisions with the sea—and fell in and out of a restless sleep.

Waking briefly, staring sideways up at what was now a night sky, the storm still roaring in his ears, and drenched with sea spray, he saw that he was close to where he had set off from. In the blessing of crescent moonlight, his landmark rock became visible in the distance, indifferent to the lashing wind and rain at war with the sea. Being back more or less where he had started left him feeling as if he'd been thrown to the dogs and his whole belief structure collapsed. He was a long way from feeling excited about who he was going to become. Then he fell asleep again.

His beloved boat lay broken around him, shattered pieces of wood and fibreglass, displaced and barely recognisable in the darkness as belonging together. The rest of his paint-brushes were distributed across the wreckage, a splintered testament to his attempt to change things. Every third or fourth wave was powerful enough to reach up over his upper body as it lay in the limbo between the sea and the land. The cold water lapped over his bruised back and shoulders, including him in the ritual washing of all the pebbles that had formed to create the shore, receding, leaving him for a while, glistening in the moonlight with the stones, shingle and sand, and then crashing back towards his world. In what seemed like a never-ending exchange, the sea absorbed pain and information from him to drag back into its aeons of rain and tides, rushing back in an oracle of insight that made dream-like sense and then didn't. Against the sound of sirens calling across the waves, he prayed in his semi-conscious-ness, *"Please drag me away, tie my feet back where I can see, teach me how to stay,"* before his eyes closed again.

He had spent the rest of the night drifting sketchily in and out of his dreams —his beliefs—images being tossed around at sea in the storm's huge, crazy arms, hurling his life's dis-mantled jigsaw puzzle back towards the shore. It went on to rain and howl for so long that he couldn't remember what it had been like before it had started. He couldn't remember what it was like to be free from the acute pain of confusion.

He couldn't remember the relaxed sense of having time to utilise in the way he would need it to assemble the fragments of his picture again so that he could work out what had happened. He had thought the chaos in his mind would never come to an end. But eventually it did stop, when he finished being able to care anymore, and a natural detachment and relief took place.

Nightmares seemed to want to flood into his life, as if Melpomene herself had seen the opportunity to write his life into a Greek tragedy and was waiting to see if he had completely given up. Maybe it started to trickle in with the rain as he licked the moisture on his lips; but he finally fell into a deep sleep instead, with his tongue stilled and his mouth left open. In his deep sleep he rolled onto his side, bringing his knees up to his chest in a foetal pose and letting go of absolutely everything before it was able to consume him. The deadness and the debris in his mind were washed in the rhythm of his sleeping, the sound of the waves, the whistle of the wind, returning him to who he was to begin with.

CHAPTER 5

The Swallow (The Window)

A DAY LATER, WHEN the storm had eventually worn itself out too, most of the broken bits of his life were unrecognisable. Some pieces of the jigsaw gave him a sense of familiarity that he would later learn to fear in the mornings when they reminded him that the storm hadn't been a dream. But they would also give him a glimmer of hope as he tried lamely to adjust to the scene around him.

There were patches of blue sky, a wing, birds, a steering wheel, crisp packets, soggy biscuits, bits of yellow boat and bits of people. And there were missing pieces. There were too many missing pieces. He didn't know who he was as he turned over the next broken piece and then another that didn't make sense of the first one. Any piece he cared to pick up couldn't give him anything close to enough for a picture he could relate to anymore. He opened a can of drink, no longer present and correct in its box, and found relief in the hissing sound as he pulled the can ring. The sweet but cold and harsh taste of the liquid hit the dryness of his throat. The surprise of his thirst connected him to the scenery reconfirming that he was human, vulnerable and alive. He didn't let go of the paintbrush while he opened the can. They had washed up on the shore together. As much as the cold drink confirmed that he was somewhere real, the paintbrush confirmed what he'd experienced.

He found a use for the paintbrush, the hardened bristles flicking off damp sand from the irregular shapes that he uncovered. Over the coming days he would notice himself picking up some of the pieces with more frequency than others and starting to build a sensation of memory. If he revisited them enough, the machinery in his brain started to see a profile. As he got used to examining the pieces, an overwhelming, deep, deep ache in his chest appeared as if something or somebody was suddenly missing from his life.

> *A stranger emerges from strange ruins,*
> *acting for a deceased introduction,*
> *and senses with his living remains,*
> *troubled strength unable to explain*
> *lest it hinder the immortal changes*
> *that conquer each day and estrange*
> *outgrown intentions without a history*
> *unsteadily walking into extinction.*

Walking and picking his footsteps slowly through the debris in evening light, he heard the swallow before he saw it. Looking as if it was barely ready to fly the nest, its damaged wing was evident between the sopping wet feathers of its small body. It lay sheltered in a sandy dip between splintered chunks of the broken boat, making short stop-and-start chirps. As lost as he was feeling, his compassion rescued him from the lure of tragedy, grateful to connect with the little soaked piece of feathered life. Squatting down to get close, he used the end of the paintbrush to delicately separate the feathers of the broken wing before attempting to handle the bird. It flinched, pecked the brush and then tried to peck him, as he gently collected it in his hands, aware that swallows were only comfortable in the air. *You'll mend*, he thought, settling on his knees into the dip that the bird had found. He was getting used to the constant damp feeling of his jeans that weren't getting a chance to dry out. The connection with the bird slowly turned a gear independently of his mind while it warmed up in his hands.

He found himself attempting to bind the broken wing, making sticky stitches from skinny strips of reddish, purple carrageen seaweed. The bird's breathing slowed down, its eyes closing for longer and longer moments. It allowed itself to be healed by his fingers carefully winding seaweed between its feathers to make a join between the two tiny broken bits of fragile bone.

Deciding he might as well stay put amidst the shelter of the debris, the artist kept the swallow warm in his hands until the next morning arrived. It was an awkward, interrupted sleep in which he tried not to damage the bird. But he was grateful for the breathing, warm reality in his hands instantly replacing the echo of sirens and grey shades of fear that tried to greet him each time he awoke with a start. The little body of breath rescued his thoughts from crashing. He narrowly managed to turn them instead to imagine oil slicks of colours waiting to be reflected on the surface of the dark sea when the dawn arrived.

He got to his feet and settled the swallow back onto the sand as soon as it started chirping in response to the sound of other birds confirming the morning. A smile of satisfaction creased hope into the corners of his boy-blue eyes and he took a couple of steps, continuing to meander through the wreckage again. The morning sun threw warmth onto the broken pieces of boat and jigsaw that were making home in his memory, attempting to create some sort of disassembled structure for his thinking. It was just enough to help him resist the urge to make sense of the jagged bits of debris in isolation. Nothing made sense that way. He tried, moving bits of splintered wood and cracked plastic, trying to see the whole picture through the familiarity of one piece.

The intensity hurt his heart and overwhelmed his mind as each memory connected to him, compelling him to remember from a narrow, frosted window left open onto the past. The view through the window was treacherous with the storm that capsized him still raging, stuck in its tragedy. He felt that he should have tried to shut the window. But, somewhere in the storm, he had lost a large fragment of his life that he needed to retrieve. Bundled memories wrapped lovingly in golden ribbons that he hoped would survive the storm. The bundle didn't appear to have been washed up on the shore, nor any of the ribbons keeping it together.

He prayed that the ribbons were strong enough to hold the memories intact wherever they were. He worried continuously about them being tossed around, soaked, broken apart and rendered useless by the storm as if they had never existed. The bundle made sense and the abstract landscape that he found himself in now did not.

Afraid to look through the window, chilled by the draft, but not able to close it, he tried to keep his angle to it as narrow as possible in his mind's eye. He knew he wasn't who he had been anymore. Without some hope of being able to make sense of what had happened to his life, it seemed pointless to be here. But somebody was still functioning, treading through the limbo, troubled enough by his discomfort to not be able to get used to it. He absolutely could not see that the trauma of what was still happening through his window, stuck in time, had set up a vibration and determination in his being that was about to make all the difference to his ability to paint for real.

He met the morning of each day with both dread and hope and not with any excitement about who he was becoming. Debilitating, isolated memories floated to the top of his conscious mind before he opened his eyes. He was rescued by the daylight revealing yet another corner of plastic to explore, or shattered strip of wood sticking out of the sand. And little torn notes and poems he had written to himself appeared in odd places like tiny signposts. The words helped to heal his confusion and strengthened his sense of identity as they reassured him from the past.

It didn't take too many days for the swallow's wing to heal enough for it to summon up the courage for an attempt at flight. Haphazard and clumsy, it achieved a few feet in the air before returning to the ground to rest. Like the swallow, he too was negotiating with something that he didn't want to acknowledge had happened. It had to be negotiated for him to have any chance of integrating it into the reality that had been so insulted. But the alteration it made was intolerable in the split-seconds that it had to be realised. He didn't want it.

On the day that the swallow managed to remain airborne

he felt momentarily uplifted. He needed more moments to head off the snapshots of nearly drowning in the sea that pierced his mind when he was least expecting it. Every snapshot seemed to have been taken from a different angle, rich in primaeval information that he needed, but too abstract for him to articulate when it had passed. The memory of drowning had introduced him to a language buried deep in his psyche, isolating him from being able to explain it.

The sea managed to seep into his dreams most nights where he was drowning in clothes that he didn't want to wear. The more fearful he became of who the clothes made him, the more comfortable he became in them, struggling to work out who he was. The fear, at least, was clear. The dread on waking lasted for fewer and fewer minutes as he got used to moving into each day. And a vague awareness took its place. An awareness that looked like the same woman up early and taking in the sea air, but too far in the distance for him to be certain. He learnt to let go of the bits of memory that he thought defined him and hurt him as they did so. Slowly, it became easier to accept that he didn't have to stay and work out how the wrecked boat fitted together. He knew the narrow window was still there, ajar, but he avoided its haunting ghost-like imprint in time that he didn't want to admit to having seen. Yet a part of him didn't really want to completely close the window and the call of overwhelming despair that lay beyond it. He sensed that he would be shutting off a part of himself that needed to be rescued, the fragment, still out there flailing helplessly in the waves, hoping to restore his memories. Managing the angles between the window and where he was, he avoided the temptation of jumping through it. The thought of that blew through the gap frequently like a cold wind trying to freeze his attempts to recover hope. The swallow was spotted several times over these days, darting through the window, checking that the past was still there and as frightening as he thought. Bravely surveying the sadness for the memories he had lost, and then zipping quickly back with a long, drawn-out peep that sounded as if it had seen something. Its behaviour, differentiating memories that once belonged to him or were shared with him, mimicked a parent bird trying to find food for its fledglings. He felt that the swallow was rewarding his compassion with its loyalty for the identity he was trying to piece together and the new picture that he was trying to paint.

CHAPTER 6

The Days

O N ONE OF the many new days that followed, he watched the metamorphosis of one of the jigsaw pieces. Stuck between pebbles close to the edge of the shore, it had been taken by the sea, tinged with sunlight catching its rhythmic bobbing. Squinting, he quizzed at the mostly cerise-coloured, elongated but irregular shape, wondering what it had been a part of in the completed picture. He continued to watch as perfect timing set the piece of puzzle riding gracefully back towards the shore along the ridge of a rolling wave. It happened for several seconds in which he felt a fleeting sensation of joy. Then it appeared to bob purposefully back out to sea again. The salty seawater, seeping into its layers of milled-down paper, swelled the puzzled piece out of shape, turning it into a soggy pink and bloated mess. It continued to float before it slowly, eventually disintegrated into sea froth.

He sat down heavily beside the rock, where he would spend many more days, tethered by the familiarity just like the boat he had once moored to it. The collected heat of each day held in the rock's density was comforting to his shoulders and seemed to draw the ache into itself when he rested against it. Looking out to the horizon towards the end of the day's time, he could never see the setting sun in quite the same way as he had before the storm and the crash. He'd understood what people meant when they talked about their world having been turned upside down and their dreams lost.

Yet more days passed and blended into one long passage

of time in which he ventured along the shoreline to maintain sight of where the woman appeared next, carefully changing his perspective of the wrecked boat to fade bit by bit into the distance. Sufficiently entertained by the simplicity of life, he became acquainted by the sea's tides. The geometry of new shells and stones, deposited in the hours of stillness when the sea receded, gave him a sense of satisfaction. He was troubled only slightly by what he was supposed to make of the crows and their comic antics when he picked up one of the shells or stones. But it was more than his mind could deal with to spend too long on any one day trying to figure it out. While the cells in his bruised body renewed themselves, finding their way back to the blueprint in his genetic code, his mind tried to do the same. He settled into a gradual adaptation to the props around him which wrote the content of the days. A kaleidoscope being twisted around him, he let go of trying to understand the changing patterns and shapes now incidental to his own internal sense of time while the sun and the moon turned the pages of his life.

CHAPTER 7

Other People

I N TIME, BOATS returned to the storm-swept scene. Other people began to appear in his days, walking or wanting to engage with the sea. He felt ambivalent towards them, but he accepted the intrusion along what he'd come to regard as his shore. Water-skiers, wake-boarders, with and without crash vests, and the occasional surfer, if the sea was rough enough. They all came with their connection to the water's edge. It seemed that there were different ways to meet the challenge of riding and balancing on the water, but the people were much the same as far as he was concerned. Most of them were oblivious to him shuddering at the thought of the sea while they left their footprints in the gritty sand and shingle. They were usually too preoccupied, tip-toeing to avoid sharp bits of stone from hurting their bare feet before wading into the world that had crashed him.

It was an unpredictable world where a surfer could connect a board to the water assuming it would hold steady while they clambered on and paddled out, pushing and searching, ready to react to the conflict of the rough water that they needed. The walk into the water was ungainly but always a bit humorous, like his black crows and their lop-sided half-hopping, half-walking. Anyone who turned up in the picture with a ski or a wakeboard to connect them to the water, found themselves trying to make the most of an awkward situation, as they prepared for the boat. There was the challenge of getting far enough into the sea to float with ease of movement, but still be able to touch the rocks and shingle at the bottom. This was the quest for poise and stillness while they fully connected themselves to prepare for movement. It was as much an act of faith as an acquired skill that it would somehow work out and they would soon find themselves riding on the sea. Faith emerging when there was no comprehensible alternative other than to not try. There was no guide book on how to do it, keeping the connection from being scraped by the seabed, getting their feet into the hard rubber bindings fastened to the board or the ski. Floating out far enough, supported by their crash vests, to be hauled up as smoothly as possible by the boat when the rope handle was flung in front of them.

And then it would suddenly all come together when the boat engine started and the stretched-out rope pulled them up, changing ugly ducklings into swans commanding the water. The driver's patience was interesting, with just an occasional tug of the rope to check for knots in the line. Waiting for the rider at the end of it to get steady enough, positioned, and the agreement to pull them out of the water to become airborne. The familiar sounds of "ready", "wait a second", and "what's the speed?" were comforting and pleasant on the warm summer air as they reached the artist's ears.

He liked to study everybody intensely as they moved around in his picture between the here and now, trying to avoid his stare. He developed a slight sense of hope and optimism as he watched the array of attractive designs identifying the boards and skis brought to the shore, ready to conjure the unsuspecting riders out of his scenery. Instruments of motion to bond with, the connections could take their riders to somewhere else and were deservedly discussed at great length.

It was both unsettling and exciting when a connection had been outgrown and traded in for something new—but unfamiliar—to ride until they'd accepted each other. The swap gave rise to doubts about the ability to be the best that they could be if the unfamiliar connection and the timing of the change weren't right. The awareness that they had outgrown a connection was a serious matter. Knowing when they had found a replacement that would take them to the next level was an uncertain time. The uncertainty seemed to be a common and addictive denominator. The trade-off of awkwardness was a necessary frustration of not knowing if they'd struck a good deal for themselves. New connections to the water made it crystal clear as to how limiting the old connection had been, and it also brought more to learn. The artist observed it all with great interest but didn't appreciate other people's fascination with the detail.

Connections created explosions of colour in his painting. They were so vibrant that the discussion about the difference between past and present, old and new, became like offering round a bag of assorted sweets. In the end, it all boiled down to sugar and was sweet for as long as it was sweet. Movement made unpredictable connections as the skis and boards took on a life of their own out on the sea, regardless of how much practice there had been. In his picture, there was no distinction that would show for sure whether a ski was being ridden or whether the reverse was true.

Rider and connector both fused in the same place in his mind and, ironically, resolved his need to be independent from the sea. The destructive and the gentle sea where he had knelt, lost, and confused about what to paint, who to be, and how to think. He had so many times relied on the rhythmic, salty, green water to wash the paint off his brush. Eddies, ripples and stronger currents took the colours in different directions. He could do that—watch and decide which current to let his mind be caught up in and which ones to avoid. There were currents that pulled so confidently, it would be tempting to let them seduce his thoughts far away from the shore where he could never return to his brushes. Never return to his beliefs, abandoning everything he was confused about and trying to sketch out and paint. There would be some certainty in being taken over, leaving the confusion behind, and not having to think anymore. There were deeper, dark and cold undertows of water from waves that had broken on the shore. The storm had let him know that they were out there somewhere, prepared to drain anyone of life if their morbid fascination allowed them to succumb to giving up on themselves. Curious as he was to see how far the waves, currents and serious undertows would take him, he knew where they all led because he'd almost always nearly been there before. All the different ways he could depart from himself led him to believe that each current held its own script, casting him into a dialogue that would never feel like his words.

So, he was still watching other people preparing to live— the surfers skulking out in the shallows and the skiers and wake-boarders waiting on the shore. And as he painted, he waited to see how long it would take any of them to tire of the pictures they were painting; unsure if they were painting for themselves or for other people as they waited for the perfect wave or a fast boat.

They chatted to each other while they waited for the waves and boats to take them out into the blueness of their unknown. If they arrived with paintbrushes, these were often quickly forgotten and cast aside after chaotic attempts to show each other what they were painting. Whether they altered bits of their pictures or strengthened their perspectives, reinforcing or trumping each other's realities. One by one, their brushes were let go of to form the array of colourful, sticky, mucky, wooden paintbrushes strewn haphazardly along the shoreline as everyone found a position at the edge of the water. He watched the interest sparking in the emptiness of their eyes as they arrived, spotting ripples of colour at the water's edge that they'd never seen before. Colours bleeding where the trickles of paint from cast-aside brushes had run into each other in strange ways. It was inspiring, unsettling and highly addictive because the air would never smell the same again after they'd stood at the shoreline and looked across the water. Once the connection was felt, life became interesting once more and they talked about nothing else.

The talk was lively on how to control the sea and respond to what met them as they were propelled along the returning waves or towed out at high speed, hoping to escape across the horizon. They adopted the habit of crouching down as they spoke, smoothing areas of sand where they could draw movements with their fingers and rearrange the stones and shells to explain what they understood, what they didn't understand, and what they realised they had misunderstood. For most of the time, it was a mess. The criss-cross of outlines in the sand and the displaced stones and shells showed no clear shape or direction from the outside looking in. Their efforts distorted their aims. Attempts to get close to their meaning were spun around the little kernels of frustration till the meaning was completely cocooned and lost to their memory. And then, occasionally, the frustration of trying to explain and understand each other led to happy agreement fluttering between them without any more words being spoken. The artist observed and listened, and pondered on whether it was worth trying to talk about something that could only be experienced when the words to describe it didn't seem to exist. The less he spoke, the more he realised how little of his awareness was insured with words that could describe it to anyone else. He continued to watch the other people on 'his' shore struggling to converse with the little bit of themselves that was possible to articulate, not really knowing where they were in connection to each other. Eavesdropping on their conversations kept his mind off himself and a gnawing ache in his shoulders that vied for his attention. He noticed the waves and undercurrents of their conversation and the pigments of posturing, bonding to the colours in his painting. All the time, they seemed unaware of the effect they were having on each other, the tribal ceremony between them and the convergence of the picture they appeared in together.

The surfers made an art out of waiting with uncertainty in the shallows and preparing for the next wave big enough to bring them alive, swelling up from the depths. It was the first thing they thought about when they woke up and checked the weather conditions. They chose with care the waves that would carry them through the day, integrate their existence with the world. If they were in the water, it was all about choices. It required them to at least choose the waves they didn't want. Skiers and wake-boarders were impatient to escape from the shore, constantly running from time. They needed the propulsion of the boat to bring them to life, rearranging the sea into the peaks and troughs that didn't already exist. He tried not to be critical of the boats, or how they were driven, just because he'd crashed his. Everybody seemed to like the sea, and it kept him vicariously entertained.

He wasn't sure why, but he enjoyed the chatter of other people and found it comforting. Behind his invisible glass wall, he wondered when, where and why exactly he had assumed that there was no point in being a part of other people's pictures. The chat served the purpose of encouraging each other to try increasingly daring manoeuvres that would take them to the other side of their fear, where it felt better than it felt to not try and to not know. They used the stones and shells to demonstrate the only just bearable tension of staying in the moment as they maintained their balance, crossing or sliding along the wakes or taking off without being sure of how they would land. It was where their hope and fear would collide in the energy that joined spirit and the material world, knowing that the future depended on them being there in the moments. In this brief ceremonial meeting of the here and now that held all their unrealised potential, time stopped for them. When they committed to the moment they were risking, feathery splashes of water enjoyed it with them, soaring like a flock of flamingos taking off to celebrate. It was just that once the adrenalin had subsided and they'd relived it and talked it to death, the life in between the moments of celebration lost its value. Apart from, of course, that it offered them time to recover and plan for the next moment. Striving for the unbearable happiness that kept them on its edge and free of fear had some enjoyment within the purpose of the gaps; unless they started to sag. At best, the sags gave them the experience of a boring contrast to enable the sensation of joy to be palpable. At their very worst, they were terrifying passages of fiction where they didn't feel alive. *Ah, yes,* he thought, *the contrast.* The contrast where he imagined how relieved he would feel to be freed from his present discomfort and grateful for the dissatisfaction that kept him imagining that moment.

CHAPTER 8

The Mirrors

PEOPLE CONTINUED TO come and go in his picture, with or without connections to the sea. They mirrored each other's perception of the sea and themselves, discovering what they really valued when they looked at their reflections in the mirrors they held up to each other. Producing snapshots of themselves and their lives, there was so little time to take an interest as to who anyone really was. It was reminiscent of those detectives in the old movies who flip open their wallet to show pocket-size photos of their loved ones by way of an introduction. His mind wasn't up to it, weary from its own nature of continuously needing to judge and compare, convince and modify, sabotaging a contrasting need to connect and trust. Responding to people with little spirals of emotion swirling up or down, to the right or the left, mixing paint for each other's pictures, from feelings and reactions in the myriad of mirrors. No, he was far away from being able to join in.

Observing other people made the artist realise that everybody needed an image of themselves to feel enthusiastic about—it was something he didn't have any more. Somewhere in the race to evolve, he'd lost sight of who he was—or let others take it from him. He had no image to start a conversation with, to compare himself to others, the confidence and the innocence of enthusiasm to bring life to his picture. He kept watching and noticing how other people responded to being shown photos and reinforced or dismissed each other's images when there were too many of them wanting acknowledgement for the same image. No amount of self-reflection seemed to reassure them as much as the dependency on scanning each other's faces for the tiniest hint of admiration, envy, support or uneasiness to get validation of where they were, relative to each other. Their encounters required them to adopt a role, sometimes choosing from a wardrobe of clothes they didn't want to wear right then or even like that much. The shore was littered with cast-off items of clothing and second-hand outfits as everybody tried to work out what to wear and who they were in bits and pieces of interaction with each other.

He'd lost the crust that had once formed itself around his mind, barnacles of constant judgements and microscopic opinions to help him interact. It had broken off in rough coral-like chunks during the storm that had crashed him, rendering him useless to reinforce the roles that people wanted to adopt.

He couldn't respond when they prompted him to read the corresponding scripts they had offered him, or the clothes they needed him to wear. He didn't know why he was like this, but he almost enjoyed avoiding everyone's attempt to paint with the images they wanted to have of him. The oneness of his nothingness and disassociation had become safe and comfortable. He might as well have been invisible, incapable of providing any scaffolding to anybody. He was a smeared and broken mirror that they couldn't see any reflection of themselves in, which was perturbing. It was also immensely frustrating that he didn't seem to appreciate how they needed him to be, to enable them to rehearse and project their images.

His empty nothingness held him so captive that, if it had existed, he wouldn't have pressed a button to either escape or disappear altogether. It was this that had intrigued the woman and kept her waiting on the shore, toying with the strings of her guitar, believing he must have arrived there for a purpose that needed to be inspired.

He quietly realised and witnessed the necessity to feel unique and important to stand any chance at all out on the water. *Everybody needs to know they're important*, he thought to himself, reflecting about the wrecked boat, his own survival, and whether he would ever feel truly alive again. His troubled, withdrawn thinking had shrunken his world smaller and safer as he retrieved his understanding of where he was. What he'd regarded as his own patronising tolerance towards his human condition was being replaced with something, he guessed, people would describe as humility. He suspected that he was no different to other people really. And he was painfully aware that he could only be unique by virtue of everybody else…just as long as they didn't get too close. Undefined by anybody, he slowly accepted that he needed other people. But his disinterest in having opinions had loosened his attachment to them. So, they were quick to give up, failing to make a connection to him. Nonetheless, whether they realised it or not, they became props in the scenery of his shattered life and creativity. He needed them more than they needed him.

This was how he'd remained, disconnected since the boat crash, trying to repaint his life, mixing his feelings to spiral in different directions, creating new colours. He liked the disconnection, but he wasn't sure if he was really alive anymore or which was more real—his ordinariness or the frightening eccentricity that kept him remote and painting.

It came to pass that he was only noticeable because of his lack of reaction to the activity from other people. He determinedly continued to avoid the impact of their projected images and perceptions of him that he didn't like. "Others have to still be there," he acknowledged, "otherwise I can't be here." Everyone who encountered him on the shore eventually gave in and left him alone as far as possible.

He learnt from them, watching as they took it in turns to fulfil or push beyond the images of themselves flying, spinning on the waves or wakes, churned up by the boat, or cutting through them on the knife-edge of a ski. The bonds between those that were compatible with each other's images grew more reliant on mutual tolerance and the perspective they needed to feel alive. They valued the sanctuary of shared moments and understanding between each other, carefully achieved by virtue of gluing their judgements and decisions together to build up the crustiness. It helped them

56

to avoid the gravitational pull of the familiar, spiralling assumptions they might otherwise make. Every word, every smile and every loyalty strengthened the reality they were building together in the hope that it was real enough to live.

They talked about the challenge obsessively, never quite able to command it as a reality from the safety of the shore. It warmed his soul, heart and mind like gooey, runny honey to hear them laughing and enjoying each other's banter, encouraging each other to be more than they were as they waited at the edge of the sea.

And when their wave or boat arrived, everything they talked about was instantly forgotten as, one by one, they waded deeper into the reassuring seawater for their baptismal challenge. All their talking and obsessing was abandoned on the shore, sifted between the stones and shells they'd used to help them communicate what was so difficult to put into words. The great thing about the waves and the boat was that everybody's mirroring was forgotten. There was only the reality of the here and now that the waves or the boats pulled them into, forcing a reaction. Last-minute thoughts were left swirling around in the water as skiers rose quickly out of it, gripping the handle that the driver had thrown to them. Time on the water was a chance to experience what thinking prevented. The reality of a ski or board connecting with the sea was the sum total of all their hopes and fears. It could be as unnerving as asking to have your future told. It could be disappointing or surprising when their bodies didn't respond the way they expected once they were drawn up onto the water or stood up on a board. The experience could never be exactly as planned. It allowed them to dilate time and find stillness in the movement the boat had helped them to become a part of. They might have lived that moment a hundred times in their minds. On the rare days that it coincided with what they actually felt, it was cause for celebration. Back on the shore, they would dry off, light fires with driftwood, drink cool golden beer and let their minds calm with the setting sun, waiting for the gaps to return.

Discarded intentions, laced around the fire site, gleamed to catch their attention while they tried to work out the separation from what they had hoped to achieve. The reality they escaped from became increasingly difficult to return an interest to. Taking turns to nudge the spitting flames, the splinters of driftwood kept them warm for as long as the conversation continued to keep them on the shore. When dusk arrived, the firelight often revealed small pieces of his jigsaw jutting out of the disturbed sand and stones around the fire. It was so incredibly satisfying for him to watch them pick up a piece of his puzzle, brush the sand off, and for him to recognise it as a missing part of his picture.

They intrigued him as he wondered about the difference each of them made to everything as they chose to move or stay still. In the mesmerising flickers of flames—the evening brought moths, dragonflies, and other winged things glinting and darting around their heads—they felt happy and at peace with their day. Feeling defined and renewed by their choices, they were always glad they had decided to get out on the water again, regardless of what had happened. It increased their realisation of what was possible as the tide of adrenaline that had flooded their brains remained just long enough to shift the structure of their thinking before quietly seeping away again. Their need to reinforce each other's reality deeply affected the artist. He developed an increasing dependence on the woman as his interest in changing his future grew.

CHAPTER 9

The Connections

H E TRIED TO capture these days in his mind, holding them as still as he could, and long enough to sketch out the impressions for his work in progress. He squinted to position the board riders into twisted shapes and tossed them into the blue skies of his mind for snapshots. He leant his head to one side, adding touches of colour here and there, deepening contours, tilting skiers a little in one direction or the other until they were virtually horizontal to the water and drenched in rejuvenating droplets. He gently tipped their angles and poses when they coincided with other riders, curious to see how it modified the moment and the reactions they got from the audience they provided each other with. He liked to anticipate whose attention was being sought, and who needed somebody—not just anybody—to notice. He was good at it, almost reassured as he noticed people arriving into the scene right on cue, identifying whose eyes they needed to catch, connect and exchange information with.

It kept him distracted for as long as there was a piece of the scene that he couldn't quite hold steady for long enough to examine properly. He sifted through the array of images for inspiration, looking for the perfect picture to paint and the perfect moment to feel. Little did he know of the effect he was having on those he watched riding on the sea, and straying in and out of the scenery. They rarely bothered with him anymore which was how he liked it. He'd forgotten what it was like to have anybody take an interest in him until the muse had appeared, and she was enough for him.

He thought that his weary need to not have anybody adjusting their existence around him would allow him to go unnoticed for as long as he liked, blending into the background. Nobody trying to elicit his attention, a glimmer of approval, a reaction from him that would match the perception they had of themselves. He liked feeling free of the need to decide how to respond, avoiding default behaviour that he'd outgrown before he was clear about who he could possibly be now. He'd assumed, wrongly, that his aversion to making connections would keep him invisible in the hall of mirrors. He'd hoped everyone would go on forever to be too busy to notice what wasn't real to him anymore, distracted, fulfilling each other's expectations about what was important.

But, instead, ironically in his isolation, he'd become a source of intrigue to those who had been drawn to the shore and lingered. They were awkward around him, no longer trying to evoke a reaction. To them, he was always there, watching, sketching, caught between the water and the land, impossible to understand. He seemed unbothered about what perception they had of him and didn't take part in the usual negotiation and testing.

They could see that his shoulders bothered him. His methodical shrugging coincided with a look of controlled acceptance of discomfort, making him look a little older than his youthful years. Their soothing and sympathetic noises were met with indifference. They couldn't find any vulnerability in him to put them at ease when they started to sense his potential to change their picture. It unnerved them, not knowing what he wanted, being unable to work out who they were in relation to him and how to establish some mutual social currency with him. There were no clues as to what he was interested in. So they were never sure if they were missing out on something as they tried to follow the line of his gaze. He was well aware that they were working out ways to build the trust that would enable them some bargaining power, but he wasn't in the market to buy it.

From the safety of his stillness, he watched them dashing around. Like children chasing dragonflies, which they occasionally caught, ironically it seemed, as they tried to understand the ability to fly. He used the time to draw on how they shaped each other's optimism and hope, guilt and doubt, persuading each other to stand in different places and change their perspectives and perceptions. He watched egos being flipped around in a pinball machine of social bargaining as everybody tried to find themselves through each other and feel comfortable. The hard whack of the flippers kept them moving through the game's machinations so that nobody felt comfortable for too long.

The stickiness of connections to other people and their need for each other to confirm their existence bothered him like the overly sweet taste of jam stuck on his teeth. It had become less awkward and painful to completely avoid the bonds and exchanges of conversation that he couldn't attach himself to—didn't want to be defined by. It wasn't so much that he didn't care about what interested them, he just didn't want to be influenced—or questioned—as he struggled with his painting. He saw the purpose of words before they were spoken, and his interests remained a challenge for anyone to guess. He was hidden, disguised, in garb that he didn't feel comfortable in, shedding personalities like cast-off clothing for the wind to blow around. And so it went on, with him avoiding the need to feel or attach to anything, no one daring to risk disturbing him too much, and little seeming to change from one day to the next. His interests were always so well camouflaged by the future that nobody ever noticed the muse and how much she inspired him. That was how he needed it to stay with everybody posed until he'd worked out the composition for his picture.

He made them feel uncomfortable when he looked towards them like a heron staring into the water, deliberating over which thoughts to keep and which ones to let go of. Some would occasionally stop to look at the sea with him, questions they daren't ask swimming around in their heads. Nearly a year of days passed by, and they lost interest in trying to remember when and how he had ended up in their picture. It never occurred to them that they might be in his picture. That they wandered in and out and between the pictures of lives juxtaposed with theirs and sometimes didn't return in time. Or that they might have been included in one of his pencilled sketches that ended up mangled into another screwed-up bit of paper dropped at his feet.

Standing still for too long, studying and being studied, wasn't good for him. The strain of it made the pain in his shoulders worse as he thought too much about what was missing. He thought that if he rested from the arena of emotional responses, he would know, and be, exactly what he was. But for as long as he remained distant, still and unconnected to anything that needed a response, he was exactly all he could be.

Safe on the shore, he could continue to contemplate the gaping sense of what was missing. He could hold the moment so well in his mind, some people never realised he was there. Attracted by the space he'd created with his detachment, they continued to wander through his painting without knowing it. He continued to tolerate the reminder that other people existed and that he needed them.

Occasionally, as they gathered at the water's edge, he had noticed a paintbrush in their hand or pocket, ready for painting. Sometimes, they would stop to fit a piece of unearthed jigsaw into his puzzle while he just stared at them—taking in the detail for his painting and slowly realising that the people around him might be creating a life for him. There had been many days like that, with testing fingers trying to piece the complementary outline of a tiny bit of cardboard into one of the spaces in his head. Most of the time it irritated him, watching people turning a piece between their fingers as they contemplated whether to attempt to fit it into his picture. He usually knew before they did whether it was going to fit, and resented the brief connections that were made as he begrudgingly allowed his life to be rebuilt with the help of others.

The background of his painting started to layer with the permissions and restrictions in his interactions with other people. A landscape of uncertainty, it manifested as a general level of mutually acceptable choices and limitations. He realised how difficult it was for people to have an identity without it mattering to someone else.

So, while they weren't looking, he surreptitiously gathered back the pieces of trust he had lost by inadvertently believing he had to give it away and share responsibility for it with others. As he did so, the fear of being let down by anybody but himself disappeared and he felt lighter, something close to complete, more brightly coloured, his mind vibrating new energy.

CHAPTER 10

The Shoreline

O N ROUGH DAYS, surfers appeared wishing and hoping with their boards, pushing them out into the sea and waiting to coincide with the right wave. Eventually, almost always, he would see them returned to the shore like driftwood. Back at the shore where everything felt familiar, he watched them stagger excitedly out of the water and steady themselves on the uneven stones before propping their beautiful connections to somewhere different safely in the sand. They swapped stories about how close they had come to going beyond themselves. Whether disappointed or inspired to try again, the sea was never out of their minds. Not everyone wanted to try to paint. They stayed on the shore, observing, or they went in and connected to the sea, and that was okay. Some painted even though they weren't artists. Some were artists and had no choice but to paint, and occasionally, they found themselves in the sea too.

He understood why some of the people that came to the shore never picked up a paintbrush in the first place. The sea was the most difficult thing he had ever tried to paint. Every attempt to capture it (with soft or hard strokes of his brush) made it look less like what it was, less real, unless he squinted and held it at arm's length. The fussing and fiddling with the painting had diminished as it took on a life of its own and he tried less and less to control it. The more accurate he was in capturing what he saw, the less real it looked. The sketching of ideas or studies, such as how water droplets were constructed, had gradually slowed down, with him becoming bored with the point of it. He preferred to paint an impression of what he saw and how it made him feel, so it became a part of him.

On calmer days that were no good to the surfers, boats would arrive to take the skiers and wake-boarders out near the horizon before they too were returned close to where he stood. The boats never came quite close enough for him to make out who was driving. He would quickly sketch an impression of the driver in his mind before the boat pulled its riders out towards the horizon…or when it brought them back. And so it went on. Sometimes, the boats returned alone. The artist was puzzled, but the driver seemed unbothered with wherever they might have vanished to.

Most of all, he felt drawn and compelled to watch the skiers. As the speedboats whipped them rhythmically from side to side, they gracefully released a hand from the rope handle, alternating on the turns to set up a counterbalance for the change of their ski edge, stretching their torsos to be more than they were before crossing the wake in the other direction. When they returned to his eyesight, they skimmed into the shoreline like swans landing on water. The speeding boat would suddenly veer at the last minute to avoid grounding itself in the shallows, whiplashing the skier, ready to let go of the rope, past itself to arrive back on the shoreline. The skiers shone with exhilaration as they dropped to their knees once back on dry land.

On the very calmest of summer days, if he pushed his brush into the fluffy white clouds, he could slowly stir the paint and smooth it into a perfect moment of milky blueness for them to ski under. On days like that, his skiers seemed to almost fly as they let go of the rope handle with one hand, streaking the sky with pink and orange that momentarily appeared to transform into sunlit birds in his perfect sky before the colours dissolved. It lessened his boredom and brought him closer to working out what he needed. Other people had become part of his painting in one way or another, and he was pleased they were there.

CHAPTER 11

The Ski

I T WAS ON one of those calm days when he was feeling indifferent as to whether he would ever venture into
the sea again or become wedded to the land that he met
somebody not unlike himself—another artist. He'd let go of
a few more sketches in quick succession, enjoyed scrunch-
ing the paper into little balls, then kept his eyes on them as
the breeze sent them rolling delicately along the shore like
tumbleweed. It felt decisive enough for him to consider that
he could stay safe where he was forever with a constant
reminder from the sea that he could be different. He caught
fleeting glimpses of how he used to be, carried in the waves
dissipating happily onto the shore. In those times, he liked
knowing that he had options more than he liked making
decisions.

He was lost and found at the beginning and the end of
where the land and sea met and parted from each other. Forever separated to allow each other to exist, he couldn't think
of a better place to be than somewhere between the movement and the stillness. Sketching attempts to join everything
together he concluded that, theoretically, the sea must eventually win as it eroded the land. The thought worried him as
he screwed up more bits of paper and let them drop skitter-
ing across the sand with his other tumbleweed in the breeze.

Looking up, as another artist tried to avoid tripping over
his tumbleweed sketches, he hadn't been able to hide his
amusement at her stumbling into his picture. It was the first
time his curiosity had been stirred by anyone other than the
mysterious muse that appeared in his days. There was noth-

ing mysterious about the very real and clumsy woman now standing in front of him. She too seemed surprised to see him, as if she hadn't noticed he was there until he smiled. He smiled because he didn't know what else to do. In one hand, she carried a paintbrush dripping pink, orange and gold onto his sand and stones. And in her other hand, she had been carrying the most beautifully balanced ski he had ever seen anybody painted with. He could forever shut his eyes to recall how the hazy sunlight had fallen like soft petals on its exquisite, rose-coloured artwork as she came easily into focus. It took him by surprise to realise how fuzzy everybody else in the painting was compared to her, despite having worked so hard for so long to find shape and definition in everything around him.

Turning himself inside out, searching for something different, he'd almost defined himself in the way he did or mostly didn't connect to the others in his picture. It was intensely enjoyable when he identified the need for some outline around somebody's elbow, calf, cheekbone, or the shadow created by a well-defined muscle. Sure, he enjoyed the blending and impressionistic effects. But it satisfied him to be able to bend and press the paintbrush tip more firmly into an edge to leave a clearer, darker line or shadow for contrast. The constant refining of the contrast to define his picture drew his eyes to the relief of light and the spaces between the contours.

Now, standing there in front of him with the sunlight turning her eyes to mirrors, she was clearer than anyone he'd ever met. She was too real for him to take her all in and not feel a little overwhelmed. Pushed into the loose waistband of her cut-down denim shorts, he noticed a tube of ochre oil paint. And above her left eyebrow, a streak of dried yellowy gold paint was evidence of where she'd tried to push her hair away from her eyes. The fine hairs on his arm prickled with electricity as their ideas for a painting started to fuse, and disturbance was triggered between them.

She stopped in front of him, and took a step backwards, reminded that artists didn't and couldn't change their pictures for anyone. At the same time, he noticed the mess she was already creating with her ideas that were so different from his. Keeping an intuitive distance from him, unsure of what to say next, she started to gently kick the sand with her bare feet.

Relieved to have something to break the silence, they both looked with interest as her big toe stubbed into the sand, flicking grains over the little rolled-up sketches and unearthing several bits of puzzle all at the same time. It was just one small decision, one small thing different from how he would normally be, one small change, but he spoke. "They seem familiar," he said in a ponderous whisper, his vocal cords almost creaking from disuse, forgetting to be self-conscious, incredulous with the sound of his own voice. It was all starting to feel too real for him as he allowed a connection to her presence to bring his picture to life before he'd got it quite perfect.

It was her turn to smile now, glancing up to engage his eye contact. "I would say I can't believe I'm here..." she started to say, "...but obviously, I can because...well..." She grimaced humorously and enlarged her eyes as she moved them from side to side with a cartoon-like quality. He found his smile widening uncontrollably, mesmerised by her.

As he continued to stare at her she spoke again to stop the silence becoming uncomfortable. "Umm, my name is Erato. As I was saying, I can't quite believe I'm here. I know - I know it's your picture but, well", she hesitated and chuckled, slowly shaking her head from side to side, "well, sometimes realities collide."

The smile on his face now seemed fixed and looked as if it couldn't get any bigger. He should probably have returned the gesture by telling her his name but, instead, he turned his eyes back to the bits of puzzle.

Relieved by his smile and interest in what she'd uncovered, she started to describe how she had painted her way to where he was, escaping sketches of tragedy and befriending fear by creating her picture as fast as she could to make it real and big enough to live in. She put the ski and the brush down, being careful not to drip any paint onto her beloved connection. The tube of ochre oil paint fell out of her waistband as she bent down. He noticed that she'd rolled up the used end of the tube, but the cap hadn't been put back on properly which meant bits of paint had congealed and crusted around the neck. *Messy*, he thought, wondering how much he could tolerate her invasion into his space. Anticipating his uneasiness with whether or not she was going to pick it up or expected him to, she stepped forward and distracted him with a half-painted pink bird in the palm of her hand which she hadn't managed to release yet.

That was when he realised her picture was almost finished, and that she was closer than she seemed to realise. He felt frustrated about when he would be able to enjoy the completion of his own painting. But he wasn't allowed to indulge the frustration as she pulled his attention away again, accidentally stepping on the tube of paint, squeezing out a worm of ochre that pushed the loosely placed cap off to let it squirm across the sand. She might have cared—it might have made her feel vulnerable to have lost a semblance of sophistication in his eyes, but she was, instead, briefly worried whether the mess in his sense of order had made him uncomfortable. It was this unpredictable leak of kindness and consideration that indicated her scattered mind in the abstract where nothing about her quite joined up in the way he anticipated. He was interested. Heading off his reaction, she laughed, noticing his eyes widening.

"You'll have to find a use for it."

"You could do with a bit more yellow," she continued, sounding as optimistic as she could. He smiled in response. Encouraged by his smile, she felt brave enough to pick up one of the little balls of paper that had been rolling around the sand and shingle and had found its way back to them. He took a deep breath and froze.

If it had been anybody else, they wouldn't have dared, let alone be allowed to start unfolding the convoluted paper ball which she was now slowly doing with the privileged interest of a child unwrapping a present. But her picture had converged with his, and neither of them had been here before.

As she straightened out the sheet of paper, she could make out the sketch enough to realise that it was for a self-portrait of him skiing—but he looked different. He looked purposeful, determined. "I'm not who I used to be," he said in a lowered tone, turning his head away from her gaze so she couldn't see the tear that had just presented itself in one of his boyish blue eyes. "I had to ditch that idea." As she continued to straighten out the paper, the pressure in his tear ducts became uncomfortable, his heart rate increased and his throat tightened as he fought to regain his composure.

"But how do you know which sketch to use for your painting?" she quizzed as if she knew the answer, knew the sketch had evoked a lost dream, but wanted to help him regain control. "How do you know what to feel?"

Her charm was rewarded as he cleared his throat, with his face still turned away from her, licking the taste of a tear that had escaped down his nose and onto his lips. He breathed in slowly and let the breath out again before responding, "I don't have to feel." Sensing the disappointment quickly crossing her face, he added "but", and then, turning, he tried to look into her eyes to check if she was really interested to hear what he had to say or just wanted the exchange of conversation. Noticing the vulnerable curiosity that he saw had so easily been restored in her just by the hope he had offered with one extra word, he added, "It's impossible to paint without the colours and the emotions they belong to—feelings, that is." She nodded wisely, saying nothing, with her head bent a little down to one side, encouraging him to speak more.

"If what you feel hasn't been chosen, then you know it's real," he continued.

"Although," she started to say, pointing to the sea, "out there you can definitely feel the temperature of the water change in some places. Shivers run down my spine near some of those rocks, and I can't get away quickly enough sometimes."

He nodded, "Sirens," continuing, "They can be very difficult to ignore when you're exploring the emotional landscape, but they don't come after you. Granted, there are some strong currents around the rocks."

"And in the middle of nowhere!" she interrupted assuredly.

"Yes, yes." He nodded again, animated, remembering the sense of aloneness when he took his boat out to paint the horizon. "Got to explore carefully, but they can be avoided once you know where they are and don't waste too much time paying them attention."

"What if I don't want to avoid them?" she smiled. "Sometimes I don't."

"Ok, I know what you mean," he replied unexpectedly to her, "the rocks or the middle of nowhere can be very revealing."

Pleased that he was prepared to go with the conversation, she continued, "Sometimes, I want to explore where it takes me or just need a rest from the absurdity of being on the surface all the time." He said nothing immediately, so she continued, "It feels essential sometimes."

Pausing to put his fingers to his forehead while he looked down at the ground, brow furrowed as if trying to work out a complex mathematical problem, he exhaled deeply. Then he said carefully:

"I can choose which currents to enter and be carried along by. And which ones to fight against and which ones to give up in. But," he paused again, "the waves and currents that overwhelm me, and come up from nowhere, are the only ones I can't ignore. They choose me—I don't choose them. Those ones I let sweep me along because it's dangerous to try to ignore them. Those ones I take seriously and, when I arrive where they leave me, I'm different. But I know I can't stay there because it wouldn't make sense of the difference." He continued, "Why do you think we're both here?"

The other artist listened, noticing the strength and the confidence building up in his voice. "I can only really, truly, paint what I want by dipping into the contrast of feelings that I can anticipate having or remember enjoying—I think that's the purpose of hope. It's pretty hard to create without it."

As she listened intently, looking into his eyes and then back to the sand, training her hair away from her forehead,

71

she returned to flicking the sand with her feet. She managed to group half a dozen of the tiny puzzle shapes together, shuffling them with her toes. The artist, now only mildly irritated by her interruption into his perfect thoughts and perfect stillness, was nonetheless intrigued. "This must be all of them now?" she said, half-asking and half-changing the subject because it felt well chewed.

"No, there's still a piece missing, but it's getting there," he confirmed, before he sat down to enjoy familiarising himself with what she'd uncovered. Two of the pieces made no sense to him at all. Curling his fingers around them, to keep them safe in his hand, he hoped he'd remember where they fitted into his life. She sat down with him, and they fell into a happy silence working out where things fitted in the haze of sunshine.

"Well, I'm exhausted from sorting through the strands of fact and imagination," she sighed, after a while. "And I still don't know what's real."

He thought about why she was so focused on what she believed reality to be. It was more of a question than a response to her dilemma when he said, "But our imagination exists for a purpose."

She wasn't exactly not listening to what he said, so much as still exploring her own confusion, when she said alongside what he had offered,

"I think I can live without feeling emotions—they seem to have a life of their own which exhausts me, and then I can't see the purpose of them." She continued, "I have some strong beliefs that ought to do me just fine instead."

"I've tried that," he said quickly. "I've been painting with my beliefs. The shore is scattered with them."

"I've been careful not to be pulled back into the sea—so volatile—so much going on. But see, it's all packaged as it's meant to be in the end. Bits, shells and stones, the jigsaw pieces playing hide and seek with each other, making sense of chance. I'm starting to wonder if perfection can exist while I work on it."

"Or whether it's already there in the stillness waiting to be discovered?" she chimed in, finishing what she thought he was going to say. He didn't correct her, and he didn't seem irritated that she had taken his words. Instead, he seemed to be enjoying her presence and the hint that somebody might actually understand him.

As they talked, tiny vaporous squares and dots of blues and greens carried a myriad of information exchanging and reacting between them undetected in the sea air. Each word that either of them emphasised, every tiny movement they made, or controlled reaction, swerved the blue and green mosaic, like a swarm of microscopic bees, busily trying to reinforce and arrange themselves into the same picture.

They spent time gazing back out to the sea as an excuse while they assimilated what was really happening and decided how much to adapt to each other. The little blue and green squares and dots continued trying to pair them, creating an outline around where they overlapped. He contemplated whether to show her the stone, still safe in his back pocket, its presence starting to interrupt his thoughts. He wanted to talk about it but wasn't sure of how to time it.

He had been able to tell from the way her eyes lit up, as she showed him the half-painted bird in her hand, that she had loved having nothing but her wits to depend on. She pointed to the distance beyond the visible shoreline, where her instincts had connected her to an awareness that could make trivial conversation and everything else seem dull forever. He listened while she settled into telling him how she had missed the sureness, simplicity and freedom of needing to survive and how it had denied her the indulgence of fear. She could still smell it like the freshness of the sea air she stopped to inhale so happily beside him. She wished to never lose touch with those instincts and the power of survival she had learnt to trust in. That was when the ski had appeared in her life.

It invoked a sense of familiarity in him to listen to her explain how she and the ski had come together. Still seated, she changed position to demonstrate how she had been sitting on the shore, her arms keeping her knees pulled in, watching the sun setting over the waves. Empty, contemplating how she had come to be where she was, she had responded to the movement above her and tilted her head back, eyes squinting upwards. She recollected that she had never seen such a huge and scattered flock of crows excitedly flying around, as if something had just startled them. They were no longer ungainly hopping up and down the shoreline looking for crumbs and shiny objects. Instead they were suddenly calling and rising high above her. The sun's rays bathed their undersides in all its setting colours as they flew around, berserk, almost (but never actually) crashing into each other. "It made me laugh," she said, her voice now sounding like liquid silver bells, "seeing the sunlit bellies of those comical birds as they flew over me while I tried to come to terms with where I was."

She sighed with the corners of her mouth slowly turning up as she remembered the birds with enormous affection. That really was the delightful thing about crows. They always managed to make her laugh. He started to get why he'd painted the silly birds into his picture, why they kept appearing and what made him feel so connected to her.

He was finding her voice comforting, and engaged her eye contact long enough to sustain the connection for her to continue talking. He noticed that he didn't seem to mind allowing himself to connect with her or how the connection was defining him. He wasn't questioning the role that he was playing in response to her or the script that was available to him. He felt slightly happy with who he was and clear about himself while they talked. He liked how he thought she perceived him as he caught glimpses of who he was in the way he reacted.

With the sound of her voice soothing him, gazing at her frequently and then into the distance, his mind wandered. He started to remember and see more clearly the glimpses of himself, like horses on a merry-go-round gradually slowing down. In the faltering awkward excitement between them that automatically relied on knowing how to put one foot in front of the other, he kept trying to disembark the merry-go-round too early. His head was spinning slightly. He felt vulnerable and unsteady, but he was making a real effort. Each horse was similar to the one before it and behind it, the curls of their manes painted in different colours, edged with gold, repeating and emphasising, with the up and down and slowing of the merry-go-round. There was a name on the saddle of each horse, moving too quickly for him to read until the roundabout eventually came to a standstill. As she continued to chatter and reminisce about the crows, he could see the name on the horse left in his head, etched in shiny black with gold edges, and he remembered who he was meant to be. *I am*, he mouthed inside his head, seeing his name stop in front of him. It wasn't as frightening as he thought it would be.

His world at a standstill, he listened to her voice recounting how she had been enjoying the rush of the crows taking flight and the colours of the sunset mingling and creating images in the water when she saw it. "I couldn't take my eyes off it," she said, describing the intense ray of crimson light and foaminess on the sea she had seen in the distance. "I watched the waves carrying and pushing it nearer to the shore, back a little and then forward again," she said excitedly. "All the time it was taking shape in my mind until it had wedged itself firmly into the sand where I could see it clearly." She described to him how the waves had frothed lovingly over the ski, washing the silt away each time they pushed it further into the land, defining its perfect, beautifully painted presence. Her voice slowed and changed to a lower, serious tone: "I knew the time had come for me to leave where I was when I saw it."

"Did you paint it?" he enquired.

"No, it must have been lost or given up by someone," she replied, frowning with the mystery of it all. He didn't respond, his eyes blinking rapidly, as she continued, with her head bent a little shyly, "someone's loss, my gain, eh?"

The ski, she said, had been the inspiration for her new painting when being human hadn't felt interesting enough. When she had become so fearless she didn't need to hope, and the future with all its promises had ceased needing to exist. It had enlivened her with the elixir of enthusiasm coursing through her veins, connected her safely with the present, and here she was, swimming in coincidences with him.

He considered how his picture was different from what she had imagined for herself. At the same time, carefully searching through his memory, he worked out why he'd been so taken with her ski and how he was going to tell her. They were sitting closer to each other without either having noticed the change in position. Diverting his gaze away from her, he looked down again at the group of irregular puzzle pieces she'd pushed close together on the sand until it became a point of focus for them both again.

It resonated with him when she continued to explain her attempts to control and join movement and stillness with her ski. How it exposed her to a rawness of doubt and fear dormant in her joints and bones like nothing else in the present could. She had seemed unbothered as to whether he was listening as she chatted on about her need to meet the challenge offered by the sea time and time again. She told him how it washed the dregs of doubt and fear out of her and—when her instincts knew it was right and when she briefly touched the invisible—it flooded her with a sense of reunion to everything and nothing and made her feel alive. "If only the moment could last!" she sighed.

As she talked and smiled at him, her wiggly, pale brown and blonde hair glistening in the rose-light, her slanted turquoise eyes had filled with sunshine. She pointed to the clump of tiny cardboard shapes beside them on the sand where she had spotted a pattern on two of the pieces of his puzzle. Inspecting the pieces more carefully, she held them one after the other between her thumb and middle finger and blew away the last sand grains before placing them carefully into the palm of her other hand, on top of the half-painted bird. "There, you see?" she whispered. "For a second, I wondered whether they were yours or whether they'd fallen out of my hand." Both of the pieces were painted with feathery streaks of pink and blue; the curves of colour on one piece continued on the other, where she could see how it started to make some sense. "I can't work out where they fit the main picture yet, but they're the same colour and definitely belong," she said excitedly.

She cleverly showed him the pattern, joined the two small pieces of the puzzle together and handed the connection to him. Instantly, he had that strange sensation of a memory without being able to catch the detail.

His mind was transported to the comfort of sitting, where he had first started to paint, beneath oak trees—far from any beach—dappled sunlight streaming through the leaves, and woodpigeons fluttering matronly in the branches, knocking acorns and husks to the ground. Their wings made a wonderful sweeping noise that he loved as they changed branches. There was a feeling of an early autumn evening and happiness between the small cracking noises as the acorns fell. And whenever a slight breeze skipped through the branches, it loosened leaves to flutter like gold dust in the autumnal sunlight. Wind chimes hung from the lowest branch, dangling all the pieces of his soul, strange shapes of silver and brass, reflecting sunlight as they shifted gently in the air. The cooing vibrations coming from the throats of the woodpigeons were affirming that it was going to be a good day. It was the best sound in the world. Any gnawing concern of being in the wrong place or time disappeared, and he didn't want to be anywhere else. He was home. The silver and brass wind chimes aligned, the breeze twisting the cord attaching them to the tree, so he could glimpse how his existence fitted together. Then that was it—gone. She had triggered the briefest restoration of a memory—and it seemed so long ago—but he couldn't forget it. He wondered why everyone seemed to chase moments to last longer.

She had unwittingly reminded him of when he had painted the picture that now lay shattered in the puzzling pieces around him. He had spent hours perfecting a deliciously smooth blue autumn sky that day. One of those days that provide an impossibly beautiful background for the turning leaves. Minutes later, a moth had flown smack into the middle of it. As he had watched it wriggling—hopelessly—with its pale bronze wings covered in oily, light blue paint, he felt a sense of relief from the perfection. He watched the moth, oblivious to its own beauty and the impact its entrance had made, till it became motionless— in his sky. With its wings covered in oily blue paint, there wasn't anything he could do to save it.

While he wrestled with the memory within a memory, he had stood up and taken a step towards the sea. He turned his boy-blue eyes again to question and scan the hazy line where water and sky met. The other artist got up too and stood slightly behind him, placing her hand upon his aching shoulder in confirmation of what he had just experienced. He let the warmth of her hand spread lightly through the thin cotton of his t-shirt, and through his skin, to connect with his nerve endings. She pulled him gently back and kissed the corner of his eye, causing him to catch his breath for a moment in which she brought him into her life. As she kissed him, she whispered, "There is no perfect picture. There is no ideal till life flies in the picture to make the picture real". She wasn't a mirror of his life, and he wasn't reflecting hers in the way that everybody else did. They were inside the same mirror—together, where her words made sense of everything. It was thicker and more solid than the mirrors everybody else seemed to hold up to each other. It felt safe from time and the world he was looking out on from inside its globular thickness. He wouldn't need to ask her if she was experiencing it too because the nature of it assured him that she was. And, for yet another brief moment in which he merged in and out of her picture, his barriers dissolved, and he noticed the pain in his shoulders ease. Everything about her seemed to fit comfortably into the empty spaces that were inside his head.

CHAPTER 12

The Boat

H E NEEDN'T HAVE worried about how to fill the next moment when she removed her hand from his shoulder and he recovered his senses. They both looked towards the familiar sound of a boat engine drifting towards them. He'd squinted to get a better view, but the sunlight had been too intense. As usual, he could see only a fuzzy outline of the boat driver in the light with an impression of inky black hair not dissimilar to his own. But that was all. Then, as he had slowly turned to look back at her, she smiled, picked up the pink ski, and walked past him into the shallow of the sea, carrying it carefully so as to avoid colliding with him.

"Wait Erato," he said, holding out his hand to give her back the two fragments of connected puzzle he'd been hoping to remember, "I think these might be yours?" As it dawned on her as to what he meant, she swung the ski round 180 degrees to face back towards him, curiously offering her upturned hand with the picture of the half-painted bird. Without thinking he took steps to join her in the shallow water, letting it seep into his thin shoes. He dropped the fragments, complete with feathery brushstrokes of a particular pink and a certain shade of blue, into her palm. They both watched them fall gently into place, a smile of contentment showing how beautiful she was.

"Thank you," she said carefully in a sincere whisper, her turquoise eyes holding his blue eyes for a few seconds, before turning back to the sea with a determination in her step. "You know," she paused, "I'll never be able to see it even though I've painted it, so you'll have to be the one who does."

Understanding immediately, he responded,

"But will you be there when I've finished my painting?"

"I think I already am," she said excitedly, "but, yes, I'll be there." It made him happy to know that somebody would see the finished picture that he, as the artist, would never know what it was like to see for the first time.

He wanted to ask her to stay or, at least, wait again as he watched her in slow motion. Instead, words came out of his mouth that said in a matter-of-fact tone, "I think that ski used to be mine."

"I think you'd better follow me then," she laughed lyrically, holding the ski firmly under her arm, now wading into the sea with a side-to-side swaying motion. She called over her shoulder to him, her laughter tinged with concern, "I don't think you actually exist without me, you know?" He huffed and smiled in silent agreement with her, sort of, as he thought about where anyone would be without someone to impress or take an interest in. Erato's words brought him back to thinking about his connection with the silent, mysterious woman who appeared on the shore – his muse. She had been far from his mind since he found himself distracted by Erato entering his picture. In stark contrast to Erato leaving, the muse's quiet presence had become a reliable part of his days. Days built around an assumption that she was interested in him; an assumption that inspired him to impress her without a single word being spoken

"Where would anybody be without someone to perceive them?" he eventually responded, knowing she was now out of earshot.

Now immersed in the salty, healing sea, she was slowed down, setting the beautiful rose-tinted ski upon its rightful place on the water, one hand proudly guiding it towards the boat until the water was deep enough for her to put it on. He couldn't take his eyes off her as she hopped around in the water on one foot, laughing at herself while she secured the other foot into the ski binding. His body started to react to the subtle osmosis that had been allowed to take place in the time he'd tolerated her presence. He could feel the cellular separation splitting across the distance that was now between them. It started to hurt as he watched her moving with the ski further into the sea towards the rope handle, buoyant but idle in the rippling water like a lifeline waiting for her. "Follow me, follow me," she said again, laughing loudly, throwing her head back; the ends of her wiggly hair dipped into the wet. She was lit up and filled with confidence from having met him and caught his interest—from having exchanged a blessing of precious words neither of them had used in a very long time. Submerging her shoulders into the water, her hair floating around her like seaweed, and stretching a hand out to catch the rope, she balanced herself with the front tip of the ski showing above the water like a mermaid's tail. The unclear image of the boat driver had an air of being unaffected by time as he watched her feeling under the water with her other foot for the back binding of the ski, trying to stay steady, floating, and still holding the rope.

The artist didn't react, watching her grasp the handle firmly with her other hand as if it was about to change her life. He continued to watch her as she spluttered, blowing water out her mouth with the sea licking her like a delighted puppy. Anxious and amused at the same time, she let the increasing tautness of the rope set her sense of direction, a compass finding its point, ironically created by her own resistance to the boat trawling forward. Then the boat stopped, everything lined up perfectly, the back of the driver's head tilted towards the mirror. She took one hand off the handle again to steady herself by quickly stirring the water with her free hand, round and round in small shallow circles, to create a whirlpool, checking the steadiness of her balance. The swirls reminded him of his uncertainty and all the time he had spent being unsure, holding himself back where he thought he knew where he was. Steady and buoyant, she was now curled into the ski. Finally, she allowed herself to feel some excitement, inhaled the mixed smell of summer, sea, engine gas and salt, and nodded a signal to the driver still watching her carefully in his mirror. Surprised by his feelings, the artist momentarily forgot his own world and willed her to hold on tight. The moment arrived, and she held her breath to make sure the water didn't go up her nose. Engaging with the reassuring tug of the engine, she let it uncurl her body and pull her up through the huge gush of washy spray, using the resistance of her own weight to bring her body upright on the ski as it levelled out on top of the water. She emerged triumphantly out of the spray ball of confusion.

Today felt different to other days after talking to him. To know he was watching was just the difference she needed. She already knew she was going to ski perfectly before she'd even started. Joy burnt off any temporary anxiety surging through her veins as she took control of the sea and cut out across the boat's wake. The faster the boat pounded through the same sea that had shaken his life apart, the stronger and more buoyant she seemed, slicing through the wakes, like nothing could ever capsize her. He thought he heard her voice again, but now with more of a question than a suggestion wafting the siren-like lyric "follow me, follow me?" as she skied out of his painting and into the future. He felt relieved that her start behind the boat had gone well but, as his concern subsided, it made way for an ache in his chest to surface, tugging at him like the pull of the boat.

Then he was sorry to see her go as he smiled after her, unable to shake off a real longing to feel the sensation of comfort she had unknowingly brought to him when he allowed her into his painting. He hadn't shown her the stone. Now that the moment had passed, he missed her like the missing piece of his jigsaw. He missed her more than he appreciated the space that had been returned to him. The isolation that her departure delivered back was now obvious to him. He was shocked that he hadn't noticed it before, like ice starting to thaw, creating a trickle of connection to something he didn't know he could feel. The residue of tiny blue and green squares and dots that they had exchanged was still working through his cells and membranes, subtly disturbing his chemistry as if she was still there talking to him. He realised that he hadn't hoped or wanted for anything in a long time, not since the evening he'd crashed his boat into the sunset. It started to inspire his imagination like the delicious taste of chocolate on his tongue, and, whether he needed it or not, it tasted good. And, as always, it was unmistakable.

The cerise-coloured ski flashed in the sunlight as its edge carved to the right and to the left in perfect rhythm, flitting smoothly across the waves like a huge, delighted pink dragonfly. All her trust combined with the rope as she pushed into the ski edge, allowing the perfect tension between her and the boat to balance her weight, creating a human pendulum. The energy from the momentum surged along the rope up through her arms, filling her lungs like liquid silver, and sending strength to where she most needed it. It flowed into her legs to scaffold her torso and bolstered her shoulders, turning her defiantly out towards one side of the boat and curving back to alternate towards the other side. Hips and knees swung sideways like a rudder to strengthen the bond with her ski as her feet put it on its edge to cut a smooth path across the waves. Stippled spots of paint in the scene connected and shone crystal clear as she commanded her movement through it. Her rather tortured position instinctively knew when to turn her beloved ski from one edge to the other as the pendulum motion kept pulling them back towards the boat. When she moved her focus to the boat momentarily, she caught the driver's eye in the mirror, and let the ski guide her swiftly away. An extra drop of effort in every turn rewarded her connection to the ski—as they worked together searching for the moments that were now more real for her than what she'd been taught to accept as reality. From the shore, the artist knew she was where she wanted to be. He saw the energy drawn from the rope into her body, and through the ski into the water and back to the boat again, setting up a perfect and endless circuit of energy and light. Rainbows shot through the silver curtains of sea that were sent up on each turn of her ski. Releasing a hand from the handle on the turns, she waved to the sky as she did so. She was really connected, touching the invisible for more than a moment and living in the picture she had painted with her beliefs—imagined with hope and fear. Nothing could stop her. And, like seagulls following a fishing boat, she commanded a streak of pink birds flocking to her side.

CHAPTER 13

The Sun

T HE EXCITEMENT OF her painting had stayed with him long after she had skied out of sight, and a tiny light like a firefly on the horizon had disappeared. A plume of pink, bronze and orange brushstrokes lit the sky to where his eyes had last seen her. A sigh escaped from his chest at the thought of being able to paint like that. He bent down beside the messy worm of yellow ochre discharged from the trodden tube of paint, now juxtaposed with the paintbrush she had left behind. The mixture of colours drying on the bristles convinced him that it hadn't been an easy picture to paint. In contrast, the simple straightforward tube of yellow ochre was warm and obvious, squidgy and seeping into the sand. "So, you were real," he murmured, as he dabbed his fingers into it. He studied his yellow fingertips and rubbed his thumb across them to feel the texture of the paint. Taking the brush from behind his ear, he smeared the tip with his painted fingers and twisted it into a point. He began to paint small flecks of yellow to outline some of the figures he had kept in his picture. Just the lightest touch of his brush created the impression of summer light warming their faces and movement in the air. He liked how adding more yellow in some places seemed to turn up the volume of the other colours. Pleased with the effect, he dipped the brush into a little puddle of sea before putting it back into the worm of warm yellow. Then he daubed the sky in several places with a watery splodge of the paint, allowing it to trickle like sunrays down towards the sea, falling onto the bodies at play along the water's edge. He put the paintbrush back into the worm again. "Everybody enjoys the water more when the sun is out," he smiled. Breathing in the sunshine, enjoying the sensation as it changed the colour of his thoughts, his on/off fear of daring to hope disappeared, and everything started to look more interesting.

CHAPTER 14

The Muse

H E WONDERED IF he should have stayed broken where he was instead of deciding to move away and start this picture, under the constant interest of a woman who inspired him, but who he could never quite distinguish. His painting slowed as he allowed himself to sink back into the past to recall where he thought she had come into his life.

He knew she wasn't there before the storm had washed him up on the shore, paintbrush still clutched tightly in his hand. He recalled how he'd been left feeling paralysed by seconds that transformed into each passing day, without being able to remember how long he had remained back where he had started. For days, weeks, after he had mended the swallow's wing, it had kept returning as if it knew it was his only company. As he searched for her in his memories, he was surprised that he could no longer identify with the exhaustion that had overwhelmed him back then. But he remembered how much he had loved to sleep. He had taken refuge in months of deep, fearless, healing sleep. In the brief time that he was awake, deprived of a canvas, he had tried to get the dreams down on crinkled sketch paper in his mind before falling asleep again in the stillness. He had lived more in his sleep than his reality, shrouded by dreams like veils, disturbing the glimpses of where he was and the flight of a lone swallow.

He thought it must have been about then that he'd become vaguely aware of her, somewhere, standing in the debris, a part of the scenery. If she had spoken, they were never close enough for him to have heard her, at least while he was awake. He had never been sure how the muse had found him, or where she had come from. But he'd become enchanted by the stillness of her profile, her air of purpose as she stood haloed against the inevitable and reassuring rising and setting game played out by the sun and the moon, staring at the sea, guitar handle propped silently against her with its body resting on the sand. She seemed familiar but, like many things at that time, he couldn't remember why. As with the driver of the boat, he hadn't managed to get a close look at her either. He had the impression of a kind face usually obscured with long strands of auburn hair blowing across pale skin. He never caught her gaze long enough to be sure what colour her eyes were, but he imagined them to be as blue as the sky.

The isolation and inactivity of each day had made his shoulders ache as he tensely sat propped against the landmark rock, staring across the sea, blinking at any sighting of birds. Every blink warmed him with the memory of the swallow, but mostly he thought about sleep. He only moved his limbs when the discomfort of staying in one position for too long gave him no option.

Bit by bit, she had created some curiosity in him as her position shifted on the shore. Gradually, his slow, curious steps had been drawn back towards the rhythmic sound of the sea that had changed his life. He'd walked closer to the water's edge than he'd been since the storm, feeling as if he'd returned to the scene of a crime. *Maybe it wasn't the sea*, he thought, *Maybe it was the timing.*

He figured that, as long as he stayed on the shore, everything would be kept in order while he tried to work out what he was meant to be doing. He recalled a particular day, looking down at his feet as the distance between his toes and the flow and ebb of the sea became less and less. Time passed. He inhaled deeply, eventually crouched down stiffly, and slowly took hold of the paintbrush from where he kept it safe behind his ear to dip it into the sea's salted vastness. As its waves licked the brush held firmly in his fingers, he felt a tingle of excitement from the contact, and he cautiously breathed out again. It was an excitement that promised, if he dared to paint again, he would want to sleep less.

He'd stood up and looked towards the woman. She had been like the tide, coming and going without the difference being obvious. As he fell asleep, she'd often appeared to stroke his forehead, placing a blessing on his eyelids, before playing a brief heavenly array of notes on the guitar. He would start trying to remember the tune, just as he drifted into the safety of his dreams where things appeared to mend themselves. And in the mornings, in his half-awake state, he dreamt that she came to sit beside him to open one of those advent calendars from his childhood, with little doors for each date coming closer to Christmas. He felt the locked-away memory and pain behind each little door upset him slightly in his dreams as he recalled what they would reveal. But she opened the doors so carefully, not wanting to wake him fully, that he was able to appreciate the chocolate reward hidden behind each one. Her deftness at opening more and more of the little doors while he was still half asleep drew away from his fear of waking into another day full of frightening images waiting to torment him. She had become a part of his days as he panicked less about trying to put together the bits of his puzzle with such urgency.

Instead, he preferred to wait and see where he fitted into the day. He developed a morning routine of feeling what had bubbled up from his subconscious to be left floating on the surface of his waking mind. At the same time, he observed his brain's reactions to the scenery around him as he acknowledged that he was in another day. He had turned his attention more to the sounds of the sea and other people coming and going. He took his time to explore his complexity and simplicity in the way that one savours the different flavours that make up a wine poured into what is still essentially one glass. Somewhere in the slower routines of his day, he would settle on a feeling in the same way that he might have once chosen what to wear. His internal world of thoughts, memories, feelings and dreams became much bigger than the world he observed outside of his skin. He hadn't noticed the distance he was covering as he followed the woman further and further along the shore.

He was comfortable not getting too close and didn't intentionally try to close the gap between them. Something had invoked her cool interest but he didn't know why and didn't know how to deal with it. It was such an unexpectedly welcome feeling to be curious, as he started to walk in the direction that she was taking. Following her, but keeping his distance, things had slowly started to change as his days came and went. The spark in his mind grew steadier and memories of the storm grew dimmer. He appeared to have placed confidence in the woman, too afraid to carry it himself.

CHAPTER 15

The Sea

H E WAS BROUGHT back to the present by the warmth of the stone he had removed from his pocket and started turning it between his fingers again. He'd checked it first to make sure it was just as he'd remembered even though he was holding the evidence that it was. The yellow stripe seemed to have multiplied in the sunlight, widening and narrowing, bleeding in and out of the bronze of the stone as he turned it around. The nick along one edge exposed a dull shade of ochre under the sea-polished surface. Maybe it was the warmth of the stone that made him feel a sense of confidence wandering quickly through his hands and up his arms to the middle of his chest. He breathed a sigh of contentment about having experienced something that was more than he was used to and more than he knew but, at the same time, seemed familiar as he recognised a memory of who he used to be.

He walked on, continuing to reflect on the puzzle he was still trying to join up for himself. It was enjoyable now, holding the stone with its yellow stripe, the combination of the rays of sunlight burning off the sea mist and that wonderful whooshing noise of the lapping waves.

There had been glimmers on this journey when he'd actually wondered if he'd ever felt happier. There was more sense of purpose in his steps since the appearance of the muse, even if the picture was unclear. He wondered what her name was and compared her to his experience of the other artist, Erato. Both women had intrigued him in how they had appeared in his painting. Erato with her happy confidence that amused him, and the muse with her air of compassionate mystery. Both had inspired him. The tunes emanating from the guitar became easier to remember. Hearing her sing the thoughts he had written harmonised his thinking and inspired him to write more. Movement made him feel part of life in a way that stillness didn't and he was getting used to it. The simplicity of his days, painting in the sanctuary of stillness wasn't easy to leave. Moving one foot in front of the other in the warm sunlight seemed to help him to remember who he was. He felt unreal and asked himself if this was his life. Or was it someone else's life? He wasn't sure whether people moved into the lives of others. When he examined the drawings he had made, he wondered whether any of the figures knew that they had been included. How would he feel if he was one of the figures forming part of somebody's attempt to paint? It was a struggle to believe that he would remain unaware if a stranger was looking at a sketch or photo of him, today or years later. He wondered how many people had any part of his existence in their thoughts right now: thinking about something he might have said, might have given them, or might have misunderstood, and whether those thoughts would change if he changed how he felt about himself.

Sometimes, as he walked close to the sea, it would laugh generously, covering his feet entirely for a moment before rolling back into its belly with a warm green smile. When it delighted him like that there was no need to think, or search, or wonder. He didn't always notice when the woman stood still, waiting for him to catch up with her, watching him learn to live again, with a deep gaze cast in his direction. But he always knew she was there, somewhere, sometimes playing the guitar, singing words from little notes he'd written. Notes he'd then forgotten about in-between his preoccupation with sketching and painting. Sometimes the spaces between the different sounds of the guitar would resonate with him more than the acoustic elegance of the strings. Her voice was like a series of pure gold, bronze and silver bells delivering weird melodies and bringing new meaning to his words. Every now and then, when she turned, she would shake her head to arrest his attention, shimmers of gold and tiny orange stars tumbling from her hair, down over her shoulders, and eventually drifting to become a part of the sand below her feet as she walked on, leaving him entranced.

Now, back in the moment, with the morning truly here, his fragile good mood started to shift as he sensed trouble. Out near the horizon, he felt that something wasn't quite right. He had lost track of time since the sun first appeared. It was fairly high up in the sky now, but the moon was still there too, refusing to leave, adding to his uneasiness. Something was happening. Something was changing—the moon's continuing presence suggested to him that an event was occurring that he ought to know about. If he could have seen from its position of privilege over the planet, he would have known that his experience was just a dot in his stippled life and everything was happening just as it should. Feeling uneasy, he looked for some reassurance from the woman, knowing that she would turn away if he stared at her for too long. But she had disappeared from his eyeline during the seconds he'd spent wishing he could remember why she seemed so familiar. Shrugging his shoulders, wondering if they would ever cease to ache, he took a step to try to take up with the sea's motion once more. He tripped, confused by a change in its rhythm. Glancing quickly towards where he had last seen the woman, he realised that the sea was about to leave.

The timing perplexed him, or maybe shocked him, compared to the usual tidal withdrawals. He had after all only just decided this day had to be lived in a way that he was starting to understand, grateful for every breath and grain of sand that completed his picture. It seemed that the minute he had felt that he was ready to start painting afresh, and feeling that he was about to join everything up, he had drawn a final challenge. Denying himself the option of panicking, he knew what that experience was like and where it would get him. He observed other reactions within himself starting to take form, deciding what to wear and how it would suit him. Choosing nothing, he allowed acceptance to fill his mind without judging it. He told himself that the sea, being the sea, meant that it had to go before it could return.

He unfurled his hand and dropped the stone. It landed by his feet, making its mark like a resigned blot in the damp sand. Then, sitting down in the acceptance, he hunched and released his shoulders a few times, as had become his habit to try to relieve the ache. His breath mimicked the sound of the sea as he exhaled dramatically, picked up the stone again for comfort and pressed it to his mouth. The solid feeling of warm stone on his lips reassured him of his existence once more. *I must keep you*, he thought. He sat unable to turn his eyes from the changing colours out where the sky met the sea, lest he'd miss something vital.

Caught out across the ebbing water, the silhouettes of speedboats, motors now at a standstill, bobbed aimlessly and eerily in the altered pastels of light and rippling reflections that accompanied the receding sea. In anticipation with the boats, he sat waiting while everything quietened. People had gone from the shore, and nobody but he was in sight as he waited for the woman to reappear from wherever she was and for whatever was happening to make itself known.

The trail of stones and shells behind him told a story—dropped bit by bit as it unfolded. Each one had been toyed with so enthusiastically, held up in the sunlight. Before today, every other new item of stone or shell had momentarily delighted him with its colours, swirls and textures. Examining them from every angle, he would use his paintbrush to remove the little specks of sand from the ornate spiral exteriors of the shells. As his brush followed the spiral grooves, the woman's interest was almost audible, wafting past his ears like divine, melodic whispers of music inspiring him to paint a bigger and brighter picture. Unbeknown to him, she watched the slideshow of his imagination with a satisfied smile and her eyes gleaming with amusement, capturing the colours of the sky. As her attention nurtured his focus, he became more entertaining, painting life with new beliefs and ideas, writing poems, lyrics for her to sing, and making things happen. The need for their connection to each other grew. The songs that she sang along to the guitar became increasingly emotive and pleasing to his ears. The exchange of their energies animated his picture—shells and stones were dropped onto the shore, the sun rolled across the sky, the sea rolled in—and away—from the pull of the moon. People came and went, connecting and disconnecting, and his paintbrush was removed from behind his ear time and time again as he became inspired.

Never quite venturing into the sea, he nonetheless adored the sound of the waves, the warmth of the days and peacefulness of the moon. The moon was always there in his life, in the early hours of the day and through the night, knowing him, hiding and returning, but always there. The constant distraction of the shells and the stones kept him from thinking too much about where he was going or how it would all end. He preferred instead to paint boats, folding them deftly with hope and setting them onto the water—different versions carrying his dreams somewhere, zooming across the sea where he couldn't reach. With lyrical whispers breathing into his ears about the future, he would start painting all sorts of backgrounds to light up the sky and speed the boats up. As he painted indications of people trying to stay upright, waterskiing behind the boats, balancing on boards, he attracted the interest of small pink birds that flew into the picture, longing to become part of his reality. He occasionally concerned himself that he was delaying his life but, from his muse's perspective, she was biding his time until the picture was ready.

He continued to reflect while he waited for the tide to go out. He thought about how time and time again his skiers would fall into the sea. Watching and sketching, it was clear that what could be created for a moment could last for longer if they believed it. The boat and the rope were like a needle and thread sewing them into a soothing simplicity where nothing mattered except taking up their role in completing the picture. He almost couldn't bear to watch as each skier struggled to attempt to stay upright, in battle with the gravitational pull of their own thoughts. Watching made him feel as tense as the moon that he now sharply noticed was still clinging to the daytime as it continued to overstay its welcome in the sky. "Why the hell is it still there?" he asked himself, feeling increasingly disturbed by its presence and effect on the receding sea. The intensity of the moonlight made him ask himself if it had always been like this, shining at night even when it wasn't needed and now absurdly in the day. He noticed his unprecedented irritation with the moon perpetuating the glare, so he tried to take his mind off it.

Sighing heavily again, he continued to reflect on how much he had enjoyed the journey to where he was sitting now in the moon's ridiculous glare, mirroring the strength of the sun which was now almost at the midpoint in the sky. Annoyingly, the glare meant that he had to lower his head, averting his eyes to where he had visibility of the landscape and all its contrasting features etched out around him, the emptiness exposed. He didn't know exactly why he was feeling so angry with the out-of-place moon.

Unsure of where else to look, without hurting his eyes, he returned to reminiscing about his fascination with the skiers: how he held his breath just before the edge of a ski sent up the silver curtains of water shot with rainbow arcs, and the small pink birds appearing to fly wildly alongside the boat in celebration. When he caught his breath again, all the pieces of his picture came briefly together, figments of his imagination touching the invisible for a split-second before it all went again.

Sometimes, his skiers would just disappear into the setting sun, smudged and blending perfectly with the painting around them. Just before they faded across the fuzzy golden line of their reality that formed the horizon, they released the pink birds that flew away, free to find another picture. It wasn't often that the boats returned alone, but it did happen.

Following the line of his reminiscing, depicted by the trail of shells and stones deposited from his carefree musings, he saw how his purpose had eventually become confusing and dubious when he noticed himself picking up and dropping shells and stones faster and more frequently. The whispers and ideas stopped inspiring him and became so mischievous that he eventually lost the ability to experience disappointment. It led to him deciding to stop writing lyrics for the muse. He acknowledged how quickly his possibilities had started to shrink back into the safety of stones and cramped shells before the wind could send them reeling, exposed, across the shore. The scenario made him wonder whether they had ever existed, while he pondered on the purpose of hope.

Now and then, a crow would stoop to pick up one of the shells he'd discarded. Full of expectation, the bird would leave it down again disappointed at the emptiness inside. But not before a brief wisp of "something" stung the kindness in its eyes as it tried to understand what it hadn't found. The crows were incapable of feeling sadness when it became bigger than they were. If "something" stung their beady eyes, or if "something" was missing, it reminded them of what they couldn't feel or contain, stored safely in the assortment of shells.

How easily he had discarded shells with the same hand now clenching this last stone in a tight fist. He was resigned to try one more time to complete the picture he wanted to live in, but he would need more sleep. He was strangely tired now anyway, an actor who was bored of playing the same role, with the same words. He had a sense of satisfied responsibility in having explored so many shells and unturned so many stones. The upturning being the real purpose as he read the little notes underneath that he'd written to remind himself where he'd been and where he thought he was going.

His eyes felt leaden from staring trancelike at the receding sea. He kicked off his beach shoes, settled himself into the dip that his weight had created in the gritty sand, allowing the remaining enthusiasm to seep from his body. The woman watched him fall asleep and then came from her place in the distance to kiss his eyelids. He caught a glimpse of her—beautiful sky-blue eyes—just as his mind fell like one of the shells he had tossed back to the sand. He thought he heard people from the boats calling far away, and then he started to dream about a heavy, drowning fish, while the last trickle of salty green water prepared to ebb away. He knew when he awoke the sea would be gone and that, once again, he would wonder how he had forgotten that this had happened before.

CHAPTER 16

The Fish

HE SAT UP hesitantly and shivered. Nothing much was in his mind. The sea had drained away from his view, nothing more than a line where it might have formed the horizon. The sky was still annoyingly bright with the moon amplifying the sun's attempt to reach the mid-point of the sky. In the stark light, he took in the drying sand between the damp stones and shells. Time continued to pass, ignoring the fact that he had stopped imagining. He waited and watched the sand as it dried and became looser, grains shifting in the breeze like his aimless mind, without the dampness of the sea to hold it together. He gave his interest to the undulating, white wash-line, marking where the sea had reached into the land as far as it was possible to go. He wouldn't know that it was composed of deposited microscopic shells and fossils, left where the sea had repeatedly lost its energy. The tiny remnants of life were indistinguishable from the pure grains of sand they combined with, but the wash-line they formed together had caught his artistic eye.

It was too quiet. The quietness that the sea left behind always took him by surprise, and yet the familiarity of it was deafening. He shuddered at the thought of walking on without the rhythm of the sea, and he shivered at the memory of its rough, cold unpredictability that stopped him going back into it. *I should*, he thought, *be able to change this with a click of my fingers. I should just be able to choose different thoughts and feel different. I should...* He allowed an album of images to flash through his mind, tempting himself to pick one—any one—

before it was too late. But it was too late. The momentum dropped, and time slowed to a complete standstill.

He was immobilised where movement would shatter the scenery and bring the uncertainty of a frightened spider running aimlessly across his life. Distanced in opposition to the boats adrift from the shore with their engines turned off, he felt marooned, still trying to hold his picture together in his mind in case he forgot it. It made any notion of moving to a different position impossible to imagine without cringing and needing to work out how he would pick up and regroup his thoughts. The cessation of the sea mourning the earth as a constant reminder of life washing across the sands of time, shells and pebbles, gave him nothing to work with. Each pebble could have been a memory or thought waiting to be selected, but his plug had been pulled out. Everything had stopped so completely that any half-hearted attempt to think, out of habit, shrivelled with stage fright.

A large, ancient, sculpted fish had been left stranded on the beach, gasping for air amidst the silence, close enough for him to witness. Washed up and deposited on the shore in a culmination of sadness and love, impossible to separate. Its slow struggling motion held him spellbound. It was exactly like the stately fish that he had encountered at the bottom of the sea, swimming around in the murk when he'd been tossed from his boat, heavy scales crushing it without the pressure of the sea it was designed to live in. It disturbed every cell in his body to see the fish without its context, not where he unknowingly had relied on it to always be without ever giving it a second thought.

The displacement they both found themselves lost in stretched taut the connections between them that he didn't know where there. The tugs were uncomfortable, painful, releasing drops of the sea in the fish's cells, leaking through its membranes. The sense of history and connection with the fish compelled him to want to keep it alive. He couldn't think of any way to save it from the past where it belonged, but he could hear his own fear and guilt luring him, wondering if he should be regretful, should have felt differently at any time, whether he was responsible for the fish and its predicament. But each of his interdependent thoughts was in danger of disintegrating and he sensed that he—whoever that was—could fall apart if he committed to anything. The responsibility of having an effect on the scenery was tiring and onerous. Time at a standstill had splintered into reflective split-seconds that were impossible to assemble into reality if he did anything but keep as still as possible. The feeling of the stone in his hand was now the only reassuring reminder of his existence, while he witnessed the fish grow weary from its struggle to breathe, wave a dignified fin, and succumb to the stillness. Another moment revealed itself like a cloth falling to the floor when a painting is unveiled for the first time. Everybody in the audience would see it differently depending on what they were expecting.

He had no head start on the kaleidoscope of buried feelings and reactions that escaped uncontrollably from within his body in response to the death of the fish. This was the only invitation to dance that these emotions had ever accepted in his lifetime. An array of unfastened, brightly coloured bonds, they continued to shoot about chaotically, with everything that life had suppressed, like a disorganised firework display. He regretted the attachment, the undoing of memories, and the bonding ribbons of affection wrapped around them and shared with the fish. With the letting go at one end, love's bargain seemed to fall apart, replaced with the pain of grieving for the safety of death itself. The missing feeling in his chest was now too heavy for the ribbons to lift off in one go as they shredded and tangled themselves into exhaustion. Coming to rest, the untied bonds fell, tattered, bereft, onto the sand, waiting with him for the sea to return. In the silence he could see sadness guarding love, powerful in what it revealed. He mourned the timing for all the love everywhere tied up, unrealised in its need for sadness, waiting to be set free, and his fear of it finally died with the fish.

And then it was allowed to happen. Everything kept safe and frozen in his heart burst through his chest as the fingers of time flicked through the pages of his mind at breakneck speed. Grief and regret for the tiniest decisions swamped him with his own buried capacity to deal with the love he hadn't wanted to feel. It started him sobbing in slow motion, rare jewels of melting tears covering his face and sliding onto the sand to make it twinkle. Watching helplessly through a window that had love on one side and sadness on the other, his understanding of the world wilted in front of his tear-blinded eyes, knowing life would never seem the same again. Whichever side of the window he was looking through, the window itself was the same, washed squeaky clean with sorrow.

More feelings that were unfamiliar to him wracked his body and left him vulnerable, shaking and empty as the scenery he sat in. He recognised the empty feeling in his chest unplugged on the sand in front of him by the surge of tears, a rich vein of sadness washed out from somewhere deep within. It quietened him to see it, his breathing becoming deeply relaxed, while he stared at the remains scattered before him.

What was left in his emptiness was what he was made of. It was an effortless strength and a humbling moment that filled the emptiness. He realised he had never appreciated himself and the golden geometry around his existence as he constantly tried to avoid himself. The window had been washed with death, and the soggy, heavy sponge used to wash it was left there, misshapen. He wondered if he should pick it up and squeeze it dry or leave it in the sun for the tears to evaporate naturally. It seemed like a big decision, with one being less painful. He imagined picking up the wet mess and gently pressing it between his hands to release the sorrow into the sand, a little drop at a time. The alchemy of tears turned to very sparkly, carefully-cut diamonds twinkling mysteriously with glints of information for another time.

The release of each drop that he imagined dripping from the sponge left room for the possibility of new juicy orange energy to flow. He started to feel it fizzing around his ribs, touching what he could now feel he was made of, slowly working its way into his tired and aching thoughts. It was better than the feelings the fish had drawn out of him. Some sense of control and order slowly started to return to his mind. He felt at peace with the sadness that had overwhelmed him with the rawness of its connection to love. The window to the storm closed, allowing one of his lost notes to find its way, drifting in through the glass just before it shut.

The frost on the window shows its outline
The small clock's ticking but that's not time
Outside is love that didn't seem to live
But it's washing the window with its death
As time waves from the skies
Dry the tears from your eyes
I could be a friend

He felt gone. He didn't need himself anymore, so he waited, wrung out with the bereft tangle of ribbons, his thumb pressed into the dip of his touchstone, wondering what happened next. The seaweed had lost its grace, crinkled in agony, without its watery rhythms. It was laced awkwardly over driftwood that seemed to be glaring triumphantly with the importance its ugly shapes commanded on the fiercely lit shore. The juicy orange energy continued to fizz lightly inside his chest, as it spread through his body. He knew his life wouldn't stay devoid of colour.

CHAPTER 17

The Stillness

THE MOON, BLOATED and wobbly, holding time with its compassion for him in a distorted, almost midday sky, was clumsily bending mirrored light all around him. It was too apparent that it wasn't supposed to still be there, looking more like a glass bauble—or anything other than the moon that knew its place. "If I could throw a stone that far, I would smash it," he thought to himself. The idea of bright slivers of silver moonlight raining down on the scene, each sliver distorting, refracting the already annoying presence, scratched him briefly. The angles mirrored back to him as he caught his reflection in a sliver of that idea were too acutely painful, so he froze it—instantly creating the space for something else.

He waited but nothing seemed to fill the space. It was a little while that seemed an age before he briefly looked up again. His resentment was obvious from the creased brow and tight lips. His head hurt and he'd lost interest in trying to understand the unusual and defiant lunar conflict with the sun's rays. The moon was surrounded now by brighter sky. It was changing rapidly and now resembling a circle of thin, white bread like those used in church ceremonies, and appearing strangely transparent in the emerging blueness of daytime, despite its solid existence.

Controlling the direction of sunlight, holding back the tides, ordering time and motion, the moon appeared to have stopped the show while he decided what happened next. He longed to be left alone and allowed to slip into the comfort of sleep away from the clammy brightness being beamed intensely onto the grieving shore. Celestial confusion, and the lack of movement anywhere, left him with nothing to catch sight of in the stillness. It would be many years before he was capable of even trying to imagine how different everything would have been if he had never found himself here. It would be even longer before his deepest buried feelings were invited to understand how the moon had protected him, kept him awake and annoyed. But they were the very same feelings that he needed to not be with him now; if he was to believe in himself. It was quickly becoming harder to scan and distinguish the woman's presence across the landscape. He wanted to call out but the stillness and quietness were too inhibiting. He panicked silently, fearing she might never return and he might lose sight of her altogether. But he felt it was safer to keep still. His blameful resentment of the moon was now a godsend to ensuring a determination to survive his frozen ability to function.

A split-second tripped me up on stage,
I accidentally missed my cue,
The mirror tilted in the dressing room,
Critical to the view,
Out of focus cameras swing,
Actuality rocking to and fro,
Superimposed against the set,
Projected characters come and go.
Reasons screech to a pointless stop,
Cut—cut stiffened scenes,
Excuse the excuse of a walking prop,
Costume bursting at the seams,
Photograph the curtain crash
On clumsy painted scenery
As the characters rehearse
Spectators' imagery,
Hardening mask, cracking mask,

Filling gaps with lies,
Dropping script like litter,
Crumbling in disguise,
Director's disappointment cast
A victim of deflection,
Fractured in the mirror's
Splintering distraction,
Scenery flashing,
On and off.

He sat transfixed by the familiarity of his own discomfort, for longer than his regard for time in its distorted form could be maintained. Not knowing who to be, how to be, afraid to depend on any footstep in case it dissolved, he waited for what would fill the void.

He tried to stop his mind with all its annoying recycled thoughts in the moon's prison of stillness, focus, and the enforced patience of motionless fishermen, waiting, knowing but not feeling a connection. A few core fragments of himself, such as never really giving up, maintaining intellectual curiosity, wanting to make a difference, helpless creativity, and appreciation of the beauty around him, didn't seem to want to change. Questioning, he counted the fragments of those values several times again till he was sure that they were who he was and that they were impossible to change. He was grateful that they'd been there as long as he could remember. Invisible crystalline vines of faith threaded and wrapped themselves in and around the way his values fitted together, without him having to try. As he relaxed, knowing he didn't have to try, he heard the wind chimes again, dangling in the breeze created by his thoughts. He watched, as his values kept him aligned in the almost unbearable tension of the stillness and reflected light, until he saw a tiny moment. The momentary puncture between here and there formed a lens for him to so briefly see everything differently, connecting him to an existence shining through it into his picture. The moment was such a tiny dot that he would never have seen it in the full undirected sunlight, without the moon holding him to account to examine the stillness. It shone through the wind chimes of his mind, fragments moving delicately in the emptiness exposed in his being. He could have touched the glassy sides of what he was then and there, allowing the packets of deflected light to refract through him and fill the ordered spaces between the parts that made up his existence. With nothing to lose and nowhere else to go, he allowed the space he feared to be as important as his existence and felt a shift of awareness into a different layer of dimension.

His focus and his thoughts were now functioning independently of each other, out of sync, kept apart like somebody holding a knife over a piece of toast, waiting to be allowed to spread the butter. The moon scintillated, letting itself fade a little more; a slight breeze was subtle against his face, gently threatening to stitch him into the scenery if he remained motionless for much longer. The chimes in his mind were swaying and aligning more while he quizzed over how to get from now to then and a safe return to the familiar. He felt stuck between the pages of a book that had been glued together, transfixed to know what was next, but unable to easily separate himself and turn the new page over. He was where people became nothing and disappeared if their sticky thoughts found it hard to disconnect from one word to the next instead of working the stickiness to manifest reality. Glued to "here" by too many futures and possibilities and unable to imagine or trust that just one movement would create "there" by not being here.

When the stillness came to pass, he would usually forget it like one of those dreams that slip away as you become more awake, despite any desperation to remember it and knowing that it was important. He would remember the momentary dot, but not the stillness, irreverent to time, forcing his brain to slow down. He might appreciate how he'd slowly acquired the secret of patience, the fascinating dimension of nothing, and making things happen, until he noticed time ticking again. Then he might forget as life took his hand and ran away with his thoughts to a comfortable familiarity. Just

like the sea erodes the land over time without anyone noticing, in each tick of time moving again, he might realise that
something had changed. It might be too subtle in the accu-
mulative effect to notice straight away. Or it might be just
enough. But it would always have added to the picture he
was painting. As he became more familiar with the process
of self-destruction, sculpting and bargaining with himself,
there would be less scrubbing out and re-painting. He would
test his picture against time and feel that it couldn't sustain
him. He would doubt it was real when it just wasn't ready
for him to step into it yet. And so, he swapped one ambivalent sensation of comfortable discomfort for another as he
accepted the need to live in-between the reality of others.
The repetitive process kept him stuck between two worlds.

He didn't really want to switch gears in his mind now and
forget the patterns and connections that had taken over his
life. But it would happen as soon as he moved. The transition between worlds hurt briefly. It hurt in the way that
a plaster pulls the new skin it's sticking to when it's peeled
away from the grungy mark left behind. He'd realise that his
worry had been like a bow connecting the past to the future,
holding it back in prayer and pain until he was ready to let
the arrow go.

While he thought about what to do with his glimpse into
a different perspective, the wind would keep trying to sew
him into the stillness to doubt what he'd seen through the
tiny hole. He could be weaved quite comfortably into the
stillness for a while, but he knew it would eventually lead
to such intense discomfort that he would have to escape.
He could be sure about the discomfort and the curious but
safe space he had found. He could be sure about the need to
make a movement. His resentment for everything having
slowed to a halt would add a hint of colour to the future and
start to bring it alive. He also knew the sea would eventually flood back reassuringly onto the starved shore, insisting
that everything be joined up again, relieving him from his
discomfort and distracting him from the pain in his aching
shoulders. He had come to rely on it—because life happened.
There was always the reassuring knowledge that the life

force of survival would sweep him along its own selfish path, helplessly evolving with its own irresistible needs.

But the moon had pulled the sea away for too long this time, and in a very absurd way, which left him resentful for the dependence and vulnerability in him that it exposed.

Dismissing the predictable patterns trying to form his thoughts, he knew this had to be the last time. He made a silent, determined vow not to forget the sea's absence again or to be too quick to dance to its tune when it returned. He composed his facial muscles, drawing in his cheeks and lowering his jaw. *The thing about worry*, he thought, *is that I can make use of it.* He felt stronger, maintaining his focus, trying to detect when the tiny hole would appear again, as if his life depended upon it—a passage out of the past that was about to collapse. Elongating his boy-blue eyes to keep his focus steady, his pupils were barely visible in the glaring white light.

As his undefined thoughts tempted him back, he had flashbacks from a lighthouse beam of pain. It was warning him to steer clear of the barren rocks and headaches at the edge of the immaterial world. Buried memories that hadn't surfaced before took him back to his boat capsizing and showed him lost images of that day. He watched a video of himself drowning but wasn't sure where inside or outside of his mind he saw it. It was mesmerising and frightening at the same time.

He saw how his thoughts that day had turned into a jellyfish bulging, floating, contracting, lit up and threatening to fill him with the intense suffering of its fluctuating, shapeless form. He stopped breathing as his sense of self split between now and then. He saw in the navy-blue sea, reflections of his limitation to comprehend any boundary around the universe, universes, and the concept of infinity. In the pressure of the cold, salty depths, his pursuance in challenging the programming of his thoughts could continue to fracture without limits and forever. He would disappear in a perseverance that would lose sense of its own objectives.

Irretrievably broken down without the resilience to withstand the darkness and the depth, eventually he would realise that this place was not his to live in. He would be rescued time and time again by discomfort calling him back to a semblance of order. Somewhere he could breathe. Feel warm. Distorted thinking returned to thoughts that connected and created. Stretched so far, he would yearn for the simplicity of being able to function. Remembering his near death in desperation, he observed himself struggling to grasp one of the paintbrushes spinning downwards under the murky seawater. The translucent jelly stopped pulsating dead in the water with its light gone, drifting. Coming up, gasping for air, he saw the grey mist and the rough sea dashing his amorphous fears onto the rocks. There they swirled, trying to justify themselves by giving shape to the shadows of a primordial soup. In the momentary flashback, he saw that the place the lighthouse beams had warned him to avoid was actually nothing relevant to him. It had never been anything other than lifeless decisions made out of fear trying to take form. It had never been a place to explore to satisfy his curiosity as an alternative to painting his life. He was missing out on nothing all the time that he tried to find form in the grey mist and murk and give it the status of reality. "It's nothing," he mouthed to himself, "there's nothing there. And it just goes on forever." He knew it would make better sense to turn his thoughts to illuminate and search for the colours waiting to be reflected on the surface of the dark sea, like oil slicks. It wasn't now at this stage so much of an effort to shut off his morbid fascination with the places exposed by the lighthouse. It was more an unfamiliarity with what would take its place in stretching his curiosity. The lighthouse could shine its beam into the darkness, making a co-existence and the contrast apparent. But there was no reverse law of physics to put dark into the light. It bothered him that more light meant less texture and shading with less and less definition. *Surely*, he thought, *an artist needs the contrast, light and shade, to create perspective?* He thought about how bright the light could be and whether varying levels of brightness could create the contrast he needed within the differentiation of light. He speculated if it meant that some light was darker, and there was a darkness of light. *Yes*, he thought, deciding that dark might be denser light and be just as relative as the colours he loved to blend, deepen or lighten.

His facial skin was taut over his angular cheekbones. Muscles still tense, not daring to look to the right or the left took everything he had to keep his mind positioned as it tried to wobble back to the comfort of damp images that soon wouldn't exist without his attention. With no more need to control his sense of self here and nothing left to take an interest in, he would simply need to be somewhere else. His knife-sharp focus spread its butter across his toasted thoughts that had lost their meaning from being examined too closely. The particles of his dimension shifted again very slightly as if there was a hint of marmalade left on the knife.

CHAPTER 18

The Wings

TAKING A GASP of air, realising how much his breathing had slowed, his lungs filled hungrily to refresh his nostrils with the smell of sea air. Excited to be anywhere but here, he started to move his eyeballs from side to side, still without moving his head, looking for the woman. She'd led him far from where she'd found him, inspired him to paint, and to write, and now he couldn't make her out. He noticed the corner of a note he'd written peeking through the sand, disturbed by one of the canvas beach shoes he'd kicked off before the sea had disappeared. Slowly, he moved his hand to shake off the dry, shimmery grains of sand to read what it said, bending his head slightly.

This hermit garden in winter grows
Where Spartan wishes do prevail
And snowdrops wither as moving truth
Sketches an indicating trail
So bare it seems this well-worn path
Lined with invisible trees
And a hanging head afraid to speak
Softly sighs where hope has teased.

"And so, the mystery of it all continues," he sighed, returning his hand and head to the safety of his position and leaving the note in the sand. "But she should be here." As sure as he existed, the sea would be back soon, and he was missing her. Maybe he'd always imagined the mutual enjoyment of the returning warm, salted water, as something they might experience together some time despite their constant distance. The healthy smell of seaweed and saline fish scales, shed and churned around by the tidal rhythm of his expectations and assumptions, always brought a rush of confidence back to the creativity that they were both a part of.

But it was different now. He hadn't seen the warning signs about the tide early enough to avoid his vulnerability. His feelings for the sea had been rearranged, questioning how he could enjoy living at the edge of its watery playfulness again. Always wondering when it was going to leave next. The moon was still hovering, close to exhaustion, adding to the perplexity, instead of honouring its trajectory through the heavens. Like a mother trying to resist letting a child open their presents before their birthday, knowing what was ahead, it didn't want to miss anything.

Something had to give, but the frail fluttering of what appeared to be wings behind him was a silent shock. Frozen to the spot, afraid to breathe, he slowly turned his head to the right and looked up, and then, even slower to the left. His lungs filled with the fresh sea air while the boy-blue eyes rounded at the sight of the wings. They were transparent, only barely visible, save for the fact that they were veined with what appeared to be slivers of luminescent bone, betraying a slight bronze glow as they lowered to hover, draped in an arc around him. They were his. 'This' had become 'that'. The multi-faceted complexity of his sadness and his love was vibrating from the different angles that had formed into one crystalline structure in his mind. It resonated harmoniously, as he moved his head from side to side, and caused a buzzing sensation in his ears.

Getting used to the repeating sense of shock, excitement getting a look in, his breathing began to take on rhythm again. He noticed that the ache in his shoulders had completely gone. Still afraid to move, he stayed in the moment, needing to appreciate how he had defined himself with a concoction of choices about what he could no longer be and was never meant to be. It would have been a lot of responsibility to be any different, panic niggling at losing sight of where he was, to become this. But there was only this now. Overwhelmed as he was, his thoughts turned, and kept returning, to the woman—she needed to see this.

He was now desperate to be seen, and she was the only audience that would justify what he had to show off right now. If he couldn't have her in his audience he could see no purpose in the wings or having come this far. She knew his picture—it wouldn't exist without her—and he felt the reciprocal nature of her inspiration like a ceremonial trophy cup, brimming over with joy that had to be returned to her.

His mind was getting used to the graceful strength of the wings it was going to have to quickly learn about with all the enthusiasm of getting behind the controls of a new boat. He kept slowly turning his head and looking up to the left and the right at what had been the cause of his aching shoulder blades. It would take several more looks before he pieced together how completely beautiful and sophisticated the winged haze of bronze around him was. Straining his neck wasn't ever going to get him a full view of how the wings really looked. "I need you," he whispered, willing his muse to appear.

Like a petulant child, a gust of wind suddenly appeared from nowhere in particular and rearranged the sand's folds and wrinkles like an old map no one was meant to read anymore, dismissing it as nonsense. Exposed by the wind, his wings spread out in full, easily spanning ten feet of bronzed glory fluttering in a muddle of sunrays and failing moonbeams. All his complex thinking of how everything would change had suddenly been made simple. How things can change. How he had changed. And now, just like that, everything was different.

CHAPTER 19

The Present

THE MOON MADE its last offering, a relieved mother brushing the hair from his eyes before completely giving way to the sun, finally accepting that it didn't have to reflect on everything for him anymore. If nothing changed, nothing changed. It finally took a much-needed rest somewhere in the constant exchange between stillness and movement, invisible now in the sunlight. Having kept its distance and exercising the power of silence, it would be a while before he noticed the departure. Staying too long in a blue sky it needed to let go of was at best confusing and at worst excruciating. It didn't occur to him that he'd never see the moon return, confident it was always there within his orbit, fading, and reappearing to some degree well before the sun slid down below the horizon.

Squinting, he thought he could see the outline of the woman returning. He caught his breath, not knowing if he wished her there or not, but he could definitely see a figure coming into focus bathed in a fusion of sunbeams. Unable to tolerate the thought of losing sight of her again, and desperate for her to see his wings, he was clear that he would no longer be content to follow her when the sea returned. From hereon he had lost all interest at the prospect of toying with any more empty shells and worn stones. In the present, he made a decision. There would be no more isolation against a background of boats drifting into shore and speeding out of sight, the smell of spent fuel, glimpses of other people skiing in a haze of pink. It was his time to return the inspiration to her.

His legs were numb, his body stiff, from sitting so still and tense. Unfurling himself, he became aware for the first time of cramp in his feet. Without thinking (and that was a relief) he moved to ease the stiffness and cautiously wriggled his toes. It was strange, like a ceremony where he acknowledged that he was alive. His feet tingled with the flow of circulation as he tried to rub the feeling back into them. The discomfort was such a blessing.

He remembered being told once that when people are the right shape, they find their right life and all the pieces fall into place with a wonderful sense of coming home. That only patience delivers us to this place. Once you've finished dreaming your life and stopped fiddling with the details, waiting and watching, it's time to let it drift off into the sky... like pink birds set free to disappear over the horizon...

In his glimpse through the tiny hole in the stillness, where the moments made sense of everything, he had experienced the total loss of fear, like a curtain being pulled aside to reveal reality. It had always been a struggle for him to under-stand what reality was. Everything he was familiar with always seemed so unreal until he wanted to change it. Then the familiar became real but left him feeling empty, with everything he found easy to imagine becoming difficult to accept as real. And there it was. Fear was the gatekeeper of his imagination. So powerful it kept the reality of the present away so he couldn't finish painting his future. Ironically, fear seemed to be the product of familiarity to perpetuate its own stagnation against the law of survival. He wondered whether he didn't dare to move because he was fearful—or whether he was fearful because he didn't dare to move. That was the thing about movement that he loved. He didn't think he'd stop to find himself again for a very long time.

With that, the sand around his toes was beginning to feel damp and he could smell the familiar saltiness of the sea. Rising gingerly to take a few wobbly steps, he heard it hush-ing. A few more steps and his feet were surrounded by tepid water offering back its friendship. It was ever so tempting to resist but he released any leftover resentment or sense of abandonment and sighed, just in time as the stillness collapsed. The sea was back.

Through the tiny portal where everything made sense, he knew the mechanism behind the sea's timing and the pull of the moon's reflection. He knew he'd understood it, but he couldn't remember it. It was just the smallest stitch of understanding but the size was irrelevant to the importance of it having sewn itself to the future. It made him feel safe and fastened to tomorrow as an integral part of his control of the present. It was the first time he'd been aware of manifesting a guarantee that something would happen. He wondered if he could find any more dots, open more tiny portals, little rips in the split-seconds of time, for his intentions to be realised and the gift of understanding between now and then to be granted.

What he might never know was the purpose of the moon's quiet, prolonged presence in the sky, arresting day and night. While he cursed its intrusion, it had strained beyond belief, reflecting unappreciated light before it gave sway. Every parent risking their own sanity to guard the future would understand.

He collected himself, seriousness across his face. Pleased as he was for the return of movement, he was determined to hold onto the moment he had just experienced and to use the memory of it to change things. His fear of forgetting who he was would usually be washed away by the sea's return and whatever it brought in with it. But this time he would remember that it had been different. He had seen how to separate his thoughts from his focus and bring his life back into alignment.

He could feel the sun on his face as it took command of the sky for sure now, showering everything in gold. He watched the boats coming into view, his tissue-like wings arched gracefully behind him, clear of the sand, in preparation for something. He could sense the excitement of the sea's approach like an underwater band playing triumphantly in the distance. He thought of how often he had flirted with the swell of its arrival, making as if he would surrender at any moment into its glassy heaviness.

Here it came, colour flooding happily back into his life with all the meaning for anything he could question, isolate and render pointless. He watched its arrival. The underwater roar was reaching a hymn-like crescendo delivering sacred scrolls into the now large, rolling waves that were heading towards him. It was breath-taking: a liquid stained-glass window made up from every shade of blue, catching the sun on all the lines and angles of water as they became animated and impossible to draw.

The woman was sitting down on the sand now, closer to him than she normally sat, with her expression of stillness. She at least was grateful to the moon. Grateful for its fortitude in holding time and the future to ransom just long enough, while he reflected in the light of its eternal patience. Its extenuating presence had drawn out the depth of his inwardness to retrieve what he hadn't yet used. A secret passage exposed in the reflected light showing him where to rediscover hope in the stillness. The softness and the weakness of its patience had shown every living thing, including the woman, how to stop being so affected by time and to bring everything into focus. Its patience had created and held him in the space, stretching time until an opening revealed itself. The woman had maintained a tension of hope and curiosity—both his and hers—to bring them both this far. She acknowledged that her sisters had all played their part too – especially Erato finding her way into his painting (she smiled at the thought) and Ourania making it right in the heavens. But she and the moon had not given up on him when he had seemed lost to creativity. Between them, the woman and the moon had given him all they had, praying he would bring his picture to life before they and the scenery around him disintegrated.

CHAPTER 20

The Reunion

I T HAD BEEN a long morning. She wasn't waiting for him to catch up anymore as she rested with the distance between them unusually close. She let him examine her tired, unguarded face for the first time, while she passively studied the fragile-looking halo of bronze around him. Leaning forward, he shifted himself a little nearer to her, but not close enough for their fingers to have touched if they had reached out to each other to exchange a note. He was slightly worried that she might want to reclaim the distance. Hoping to recognise her, he scanned her features now clear in the sunlight, save for the wisps of brown and gold-spun hair crisscrossing her face in the breeze. Searching, he saw a flicker of the comfort he had always sought in the familiarity of her profile every time she turned her head away from him. "Yes," he said triumphantly to himself, establishing that she really did have beautiful pale sky-blue eyes. A feeling that was a bit like joy and a bit like humbleness replaced and rewrote history again to form a new moment for him. What he had decided to remember as dreams in the passage of time, of her kissing his eyelids in those terrible days after the storm, were real after all. He thought he saw the reflection of tiny pink birds flying across her irises but he blinked and lost sight of them, taken aback by her looking so directly into his own eyes. Her long sunrise-coloured dress seemed to continue forever into the sand and stones as if they were one. He realised solemnly as they kept looking at each other that the shore he found himself on didn't exist without her.

As he slowly but surely twirled in a full circle and returned to face her again, the pride animating her expression was all the inspiration he would ever need to switch his life back on. There was more to his wings than he realised, refracting the sun's rays and glistening like morning dew on spider webs for her. The captivated sunlight etched the shape and beauty of the delicately-veined halo of confidence shining around him. A slow, steady smile forced her curvy lips to open and a big gulp of air to be taken in. Her mouth closed again, but she couldn't stop smiling. Then her gaze intensified, penetrating through to his bones, shimmying his crystalline invisibility, till he too had to catch his breath, too self-conscious to remember why he was looking at her. His impression of her and the bond between them had seemed much clearer when she was further away from him. He didn't know how to adjust but allowed himself to be visibly unsure in her presence without feeling uncomfortable with the vulnerability of the space they were sharing. He was getting used to not needing all the answers.

Warm water crept over his toes and was trying to float his kicked off beach shoes away. He looked across the water and then down at his feet several times - they were now bathed in bubbling light blue and silver. He was checking whether the sea really was that vast and whether the familiar pebbles where he stood were still there. He felt as if he was at the beginning of himself, pebbles at his feet being washed over and over again just to make sure.

The sea was here now, and she knew he must go. She had enjoyed being his muse but, like the moon that had finally left the sky, she was exhausted, satisfied, and her time was spent. They both knew he could not survive another departure of the sea because it had changed him.

She could hear the faint sound of the other women singing, returning from their patrol, and she would need to join them now. This was as far as she could lead him. Lyrics were assembling in his mind again, bringing all his previous work alive. The assortment of lyrics written on scraps of notepaper collected from her journey through his painting had started turning pages in her head, creating tunes. Musical notes were reappearing faster than she could organise them so she stopped trying to think. It was easy when she was this tired. The artist had turned out to be very rewarding but she'd really missed her sisters' company. She needed her voice to return home, resonating in the space where the difference of its perfect pitch and tone belonged.

She was excited to share the new lyrics for their feminine harmonies, and now longing to return to the comfort of her prescribed role. She looked forward to the unthinking movements her body would make when it was animated by sound waves from the new songs and tunes that would emanate from the guitar when she was reunited with it. She could almost hear the musical notes pinging and floating off the strings being carefully picked. Quavers and minims tangled themselves in her hair, reminding her of the orchestration that she belonged to. He'd entrusted her with the lyrics that needed to be pieced together and sung for him—about hoping, wanting, feeling, connecting. And she had enjoyed composing the music for the words his thoughts had formed. It would lift all the muses as high and as light as the vapour that carried song, and it would reconnect them to each other again. She would make sure she played and sang whenever his memory and belief in himself started to waver even slightly. He would never be sure if he had heard or felt the riff but it would stir up a vibration in his chest to re-tune the rhythm in his life every time he went off-key. Creativity warmed through him, rearranging the reality it had so determinedly broken down, bursting beyond the restrictions of his logic, the shape of his words, and tingling in his artistic fingertips.

The woman started to sing the chorus which she'd already worked out from the notes that tumbled from her hair, "All is well, all is well, all is well." The painting had been beautifully finished, whether he saw it or not, and everyone was back where they belonged. Creativity was, after all, only about everything coming together and being how it was meant to be. Or even how it used to be.

She sang,

*"Through the painted world I see birds crossing the evening sky;
Their breeze arising is confusing the spirit flame and I.
Fragrant birds so weird and free past the open window go,
On a clarion breeze now entering in to move the still and stone."*

Her sisters were within speaking distance now and joined her for the second verse.

*A swallow's heart that swells to sing lay crushed by the hand of fate,
Crying as I stitched its broken wing in the painting where I wait.
But it gets easier to sew at dusk, and the swallow within my grasp,
Once dispirited in a flameless day, chirps as birds fly past.*

The vibrations of the melody would last long enough to make a difference before they were tired of it. So, while it was good, it would be good; and when it was gone, it would be gone.

As he walked purposefully into the water, clutching the stone more firmly in his hand, he let go of any last dregs of fear, draining it entirely from his future. The sound of his thoughts made the salty drops of seawater bulge to refract the light in his future. It was ready, and he could see how the contrast had been necessary. What was left wasn't the experience he had dreaded for so long, looking out from the safety of the shore. The cobalt blue sea catching twinkles of gold from the sun was a grand invitation for him to step into the picture that he'd once tried to gatecrash. Gratefully accepting the salty goodness around his feet and ankles, he was pleasantly greeted by the memory of stepping into a warm, relaxing bath putting him at ease with every concern he'd ever had being left behind where it belonged.

In that moment, knowing that he would find himself in the movement, the woman smiled contentedly and faded, along with the fear that inspired hope with its contrast. There was just the faint scent of pink birds, roses, and singing, like nothing on earth, where her sunrise-coloured dress had faded into the air. The perfume evoked a lasting impression of her which he didn't realise he'd acquired till now. It was the joyful aroma of how things would be and should be. Everything he'd experienced about her, distilled into tiny droplets of her essence, drifted towards him on the breeze. He didn't visualise anything in particular about her—the way she looked, or anything she'd done. He could just smell the moment that held the signature of her that he was left with at the end of their journey. "Clio" whispered the breeze as if it anticipated his need to know her name at some point in the future. Nothing about the journey mattered to him more than all the power of the mythological moment and the sense it made of everything as it expanded the portal to how things really are. It only left him wondering, briefly, whether the moment had exchanged any lasting impression of him that might have created a signature in the ether.

The tints of hope and fear dried away together like the paint left in the sticky bristles of his paintbrush waiting to be rinsed out in clean water and made soft again. He had painted his life with beliefs that held hands with hope but he didn't need his beliefs anymore. They too could be rinsed out in the vastness of the sea. The urge to take the brush from behind his ear seeped into his mind and he tossed it into the water. The salty vastness dissolved the crusting flakes of judgement and confusion about the difference between dreams and life, night and day, movement and stillness. The sea was so much bigger than anything stuck between the bristles.

Moving further into the waves, he wondered about the sea. It had stolen and returned so much. But here in its movement, he felt alive. He wasn't losing the self he had held together so well on the shore and in the stillness—he was collecting himself together to be found in the unexpected. His painting had taken on a life of its own that he hadn't consciously intended, but it wasn't anything he didn't want. In the blue wiggles, squiggles and curls of deeper water, he saw the snake of a rope with a handle-bar tied to the end, drifting towards him. His eyes followed the line of the rope far out through the merging wiggles and sparkles sprinkled in the sea till he caught sight of the boat. It was waiting for him, its bright, yellow exterior buoyant and solid on the water, ready. The silhouette of the driver turned his head to follow the flight of a pink dragonfly vibrating past him towards the horizon, dodging the trickles of yellow and gold that were streaked across the sky. The driver's outline in sharp silhouette against the rising sun was one he recognised. The dragonfly circled and returned, pulling the gaze of the driver in the other direction as it flew towards the artist, hovered, and repeated its path back towards the horizon several times. The buzzing of its wings was now resonating to create perfect synchronicity with his happiness.

When he looked back over his shoulder, and through the safety of his wings, he saw the shore shrinking against the rolling watery vastness taking all the remnants of disintegrated scenery into its underworld again. The seaweed started to dance, the driftwood's ugliness was blessed and the dead fish was being carried away to feed life in the sea with all its wisdom and information. He wished it were still alive so he could enjoy what only its death could let him appreciate. The ribbons were being washed away with the fish, knotting around the death that had set them free with just one tug. How well they had kept love wrapped as the present that would endure through loss. It was a present that he couldn't open when the fish was alive. But now it was setting his heartache free as part and parcel of the sadness that was really love and attached to it.

There were clouds of dreams lifting away, and people drifting in the past trying to escape, fitting the pieces of their own and each other's puzzles together; breaking them apart, and then looking for the pieces again. Messing it up for themselves and each other to remember what they appreciated in the perfection they couldn't break free of. He saw it in one glance happening over and over and over again as they found their way to the shore, questioning their human experience, trying to paint and looking for swallows. Everybody was gathered, gravitating towards each other and away again, trying to make it through one day or another.

Everyone he'd seen on the shore was clearer in the distance without the history that had sifted and sorted them into what was left in his mind. Their lives were surrounded by large, magnetic, coppery rings interconnecting where journeys crossed with guilt, empathy and curiosity. But none of the connections drew him towards them anymore, as he allowed his mind to let go of other people's process of transition and realisation. He would have to get used to not needing to think himself into any part of it any time he chose different shades of thinking or was guided back by compassion. In those first morning moments as he awoke into each next day with anxiety on his eyelids, he would be able to choose to stay where he was. He'd be able to feel himself back on the cold shingle, stones and wet sand, washed up on the edge of the shore, lying in limbo between worlds and overwhelmed with fear and failure. He could ignore it as he rubbed the sleep from his eyes or he could return. It was always there for whenever he became bored or uncertain of his reality and needed to reflect.

Black crows were hopping and flying playfully over the stones left on the fading shore, dodging the waves, their feathers gleaming vibrant pink and orange in the burning spears of the risen sun. Their comical antics flooded him with inexplicable joy and a surge of energy that overwhelmed him with no need for this to be understood. He finally laughed and realised why he'd painted the silly birds. And the colours—the colours in this picture were so vibrant he might never pick up a paintbrush again. The palette of experiences he had mixed together was creating its own kaleidoscope sky with a strong sense of aimless purpose. And he was catching glimpses of stray colours that he'd never seen—not just different shades—and that was really something his imagination hadn't been able to achieve before now.

He was still clutching his precious stone which became all the more precious the longer he held it. The longer he held it, the less reason he could find to let it go. This was indeed his stone, a missing fragment of him, returned home, witnessed by his muse in tacit approval. This stone, shaped by the heaven-given sea and wind, now fitted perfectly into his hand. The longer he had held it, the more history he created with it. And now, in that experience, the stone belonged to him—and that was just the certainty he needed. History he wouldn't re-paint this time with the future. He pressed the stone firmly but gently into that space, unblocked by the dying fish, in the centre of his chest. It was just where it was made for. It was what had formed and what was left, stone love in the wake of the moon's exhaustion, fitting perfectly with his capacity to evolve. It was the same satisfying feeling of finding the last piece of a jigsaw, setting it into the picture, enjoying the light click of sound as it was flattened against the base, then running a commanding hand over the smooth joined-up surface. He wouldn't have realised it at the time. The jigsaw pieces were hand-picked, selected by everything he no longer wanted to experience again. It was the first time since he had started painting beneath the oak trees listening to the wood pigeons that he had felt sure and safe. It lasted for more than the fleeting glimpse through time, and he knew it wouldn't leave him. At least, that is, he knew he would remember that he had understood the reasons that led to his sense of purpose, to the extent that he had become the understanding itself.

He saw that nothing had really been missing. He wasn't really meant to repair himself so much as allow who he was to emerge. The stone was always there and had always been a part of him despite being somewhere else on the shore. The relief of the commitment—this time being sure about who he was—and the certainty of self-reliance tasted as right as the excitement he could smell on the wind. He felt different.

The words that the other artist, Erato, had said as she laughed, "Follow me, follow me," were still playing in his mind, keeping him connected to her, becoming a catchy lyric. He enjoyed the feeling of togetherness, knowing she was in his life somewhere, whilst the pink dragonfly repeatedly circled around him and then buzzed back to the figure in the boat before disappearing into the blueness. The idea of togetherness felt interesting in contrast to his isolation and the exploration of his uniqueness. The parameters of where he'd been and held dear didn't seem quite capable of supporting the next picture he might want to paint himself into. He was about to return to a moving reality bigger than the hope and the fear that had both helped him find it and kept him from it. A beautiful picture awaited him.

As he took hold of the handle floating in front of him, he heard the familiar sound of an engine, then that reassuring pull of the handle trawled him through the water. The bottom of his wings were trailing slightly in the sea's warmth as he sat back to bring his legs in front of him, raising his feet and pushing them forward. It was virtually the same position in reverse taken up by a swan coming into land on a lake, its wings pulling up and back, webbed feet using the water to stabilise. He oriented all his balance around his feet, allowing him to feel the weight of his own strength as his wings made enough of a breeze to rely on, and started to lift him.

His dream was ready now, more real than what he was leaving, as he entered the completed picture that he'd painted. It wasn't important to him anymore whether it was definitely his painting or somebody else's or whether it could do with more work. He didn't need to worry about canvas.

Not quite airborne, all the wiggles, squiggles and curls of blue surged together to push him upright till he was skimming through the sun-shot sparkles that were being spattered out to the sides as his bare feet cut through the freshly painted waves. Water droplets like jewels fell off his wings as they raised and stretched his body upwards, allowing him to feel their full and unexpected strength. His movement in this huge picture, displacing the water beneath his feet, was what he would now call life as he got the way his thinking made things happen. He got it as his breath was unexpectedly taken away by the freshness of water spray shooting around him in different directions, altered by his presence on the sea. He kept his focus on the driver's mirror, not looking up, down or to the sides. *Oh, yeah,* he thought, as he found his way to just what reality felt like, becoming lighter and lighter behind the boat.

He was completely off the water without realising it for a few seconds. It was easier than he'd feared it would be. Letting go of the difference between his mind and his body, he trusted his physicality to reconnect with the elements and all the spaces between them. In the instant that he suddenly felt alarmed for how long he could maintain being air-borne, the support of the updraft increased the strength of movement in his winged body. He knew he didn't need to think about it anymore—he was alive on a late summer's day and his wings were working. He saw the balance tipping in his mind's eye towards a new comfort zone where a weight had detached from him and pink birds had set down on the other side of the scales to propel him upwards. He was far from settled there, but he could feel the certainty that this zone would become as intriguing as the deepest unknown parts of the sea had once seemed. He felt different enough to be grateful for the crash that had left him stranded by fear on the shore, broken him down to set free what he needed to be – at least for the time being.

He turned his face upwards to enjoy the sunshine and shook his head from side to side to stir up the murky sediment at the base of his mind. It just troubled him slightly to know it was there. He continued to dislodge the sediment, shaking his head like a snow globe to evenly dilute it through the rest of his changing mind until it transformed. Orange fizz was sparkling and filling his head. It felt good, dissolving and clearing any last specks of murk and dust. When he was sure he'd shaken himself enough, he slowly stopped and enjoyed the feeling. The orange sparkles drifted and settled back gently at the base of his mind into a warm shift of restored creativity. His mind disappeared and escaped from everywhere but the 'here and now', with the sunrays kissing his face to welcome him home. It made him close his eyes with deep, deep, gratitude for the past he had to let go of to enable him to truly exist where the future was just an extension of the present that had been waiting for him. It was so simple really, finding himself. *I was just being reminded*, he smiled and thought, *separated to remember—again.*

He could hardly be seen now from the shore, as his pale

bronze wings established a rhythm of moving strongly and gracefully in the breeze he was creating, taking him freely to where he truly belonged. The boat driver checked in his mirror as he felt the rope being let go of, running his fingers through his matted black curls. And as the invisible was touched, he watched himself, flying into what was turning out to be a deliciously smooth blue sky today.

CHAPTER 21

The Beginning

A S HE PLUGGED himself into the unfamiliar, the smell of a wonderful sense of order falling into place around him was activated. His wings were his wings. The fear of responsibility for being him and the worry as to whether he could make it simply didn't exist here on the breeze. He caught the scent of pink birds and roses biding its time, rising from a sea of sadness that was really about ensuring love never died. He was excited about tomorrow being another day that he had painted.